THE SURVIVALIST SAGA CONTINUES

Well, seems like things aren't looking any better for the Rourke clan. They're up to their necks in aliens and clones and now, they have to deal with some new enemies from within. Michael is trying to be a good President and run the country in a responsible manner but when he's not battling it out with his political opponents, he keeps getting involved in family matters like rescue operations to save his wife from "a fate worse than death" and then death, Paul's battle injuries and a kidnapping attempt on his dad. Put all that together with a deceased, former enemy knocking on your front door bearing gifts and clones defrosting Mount Rushmore and you can see what I mean. Michael has his hands full.

Change is coming and everyone has their own idea as to what that change will bring to the world. Some factions want "political correctness" which is nothing more than the giving up of personal freedom for the common good of all. Of course these freedoms would be given up only by the masses and not the elite who make the rules. Some factions want to enslave the inhabitants of Earth; some just want to destroy it all. Still, there are some who just want a democratic society with "freedom and justice for all."

JTR has had enough of politics and talk; he's looking for action. Does this man ever get enough? Has he never heard of being careful what you wish for? John may have gotten himself in a very bad predicament this time. I don't think he can get out of this alone. I don't know if he can survive. He may have run out of plans. What do you think?

Sharon

THE SURVIVALIST

#32

THE QUISLING COVENANT

SPEAKING VOLUMES, LLC
NAPLES, FLORIDA
2014

THE SURVIVALIST
#32 THE QUISLING COVENANT

ISBN 978-1-62815-204-3

The Warrior's Last Stand by Vic Roseberry Copyright ©1980, permission to use. The alien design illustrated by Faith Maltese. The Milice francaise emblem obtained from www.Wikipedia.com. Dog Man sketch illustrated by Sarah Anderson.

**For more exciting
Books, eBooks, Audiobooks and more visit us at
www.speakingvolumes.us**

THE SURVIVALIST

#32

THE QUISLING COVENANT

Jerry Ahern
Sharon Ahern
Bob Anderson

To
Jerry and Sharon's old friends
Steve Fishman, Jerry Buergel and our readers.
Remember to Plan Ahead!

Author's Note

Quisling—the term "quisling" was coined by the British newspaper _The Times_ in an editorial published on April 10, 1940, entitled "Quislings Everywhere." The story was about a Norwegian named Vidkun Quisling, who assisted Nazi Germany as it conquered his own country so that he could rule the collaborationist Norwegian government himself. The _Daily Mail_ picked up the term and the BBC then brought it into common use internationally.

The Times' editorial asserted: "To writers, the word Quisling is a gift from the gods. If they had been ordered to invent a new word for traitor... they could hardly have hit upon a more brilliant combination of letters. Aurally it contrives to suggest something at once slippery and tortuous."

The term was used by then British Prime Minister, Winston Churchill, in an address to the U.S. Congress on December 26, 1941. Churchill said, "Hope has returned to the hearts of scores of millions of men and women, and with that hope there burns the flame of anger against the brutal, corrupt invader. And still more fiercely burn the fires of hatred and contempt for the filthy Quislings..." Like the American Benedict Arnold, Vidkun Quisling became synonymous with the word traitor.

Bob

Prologue

"Looks like you have the advantage on me, Miss," Rourke said without a smile.

Holding the machine pistol firmly in her right hand, she reached with her left and unzipped Rourke's brown leather bomber jacket. Reaching under his right arm she grasped the CombatMaster and with a slight jerk opened the Alessi trigger guard retention snap and slid the .45 out. She stepped back and shoved the gun into her wide leather belt. Again, smiling sweetly she said, "Now, your knife. I believe you like to carry it on your right hip." She felt along the beltline, found the Sting 1A and jerked it and its sheath out. Stepping back, she secured it also in her belt. "Now, the .45 under your left arm."

As she reached forward for a scant instant Rourke had an equally scant chance. He moved. With his right hand, he grabbed her left and spun her hard, whipping her in a circle. Almost as if they were dancing, he pulled her in front of his own body and pivoted both of them toward the man with the shotgun. Rourke's left hand went behind his back and snatched the Fighting Bowie from its horizontal sheath in a reverse grip as the shotgunner scrambled quickly toward them, trying to get a clear shot.

Rourke threw the woman forward into his male opponent, hoping if the man shot, the bulk of the projectiles would get her. Stepping forward to follow her body, Rourke slashed upward with the long, sharpened, serrated clip point. He was almost too far off, a half-inch more and he would have missed the man all together. A quarter-inch of the blade sliced through the man's right knuckles; the impact of the woman's body further sweeping the deadly bore of the shotgun further out of alignment with Rourke's head.

Chapter One

Göbekli Tepe, Turkey:

The attack came just before dawn; it was both brutal and effective. Within moments the security overwatch had been eliminated as the riders had descended on the camp from all directions. From a sound sleep, Natalia was awakened by shouts, gunfire, and screams of the dying. Clad only in treated silk underwear designed to wick moisture away from her body, she grabbed her Walther and charged outside the tent, only to be slammed by a charging horse. The impact threw her twenty feet through the air; she slammed into the ground landing on the back of her shoulders. Her head bounced twice and she was unconscious.

The initial shots had come at once as if on signal; the camp defenders were caught by surprise and with no clear target. Then the riders came and they had come from all sides on stocky horses with short but strong legs and large heads. Their mane and tails were very long. The riders fired automatic weapons and sprayed the camp indiscriminately. Bodies dropped and those trying to respond were cut down.

Dismounting, the riders drew swords and knives to finish off their victims, the attack lasting under ten minutes. When Natalia awoke, her head hurt. Crusted blood covered the left side of her face. She awoke to a scene from hell. Next to the camp fire was a stack of bodies and three poles which had been driven into the ground; three decapitated heads had been stuck on them. She recognized the archaeological team leader, Dr. Franklin, and the head of her security team, Special Agent Withers. But the third had been beaten so badly the features of the face had been destroyed. The smell of roasting meat rose in her senses and she saw her captors slicing pieces from corpses and eating them.

Her hands were tied behind her; her ankles lashed together, both with what appeared to be horse hair ropes. She was naked; naked, unarmed and a prisoner. By the fire, one of the attackers noticed her and stood. He wiped the blood and grease from his hands on his pants and approached. He was short and stocky; a heavy-set fellow with a large round head and a broad face featuring a wide flat nose, prominent cheekbones, and dark almond-shaped eyes. The constant exposure to the sun, wind and frost, gave his skin a swarthy, almost leathery appearance, even though his face was covered with a protective coating of grease.

He wore a bushy mustache and when he removed his leather and brass helmet she saw his head was shaved, except for the straight black hair on the sides of his head which he braided and looped up behind his ears. He wore a tunic which was open from top to bottom, folded over the breast, and fastened on the right side. It appeared to be made from a coarse cotton or hemp cloth and stiffened with a glue-like substance to hold its form. His stench was suffocating; his clothes appearing to have never been washed. The smell of burned meat, grease, blood, and body odor overwhelmed her.

He wore his trousers tucked into his boots; they appeared to be made of a stubby felt or leather. She noticed several of the others had strapped their trousers at the ankles instead of tucking them into their boots. He knelt in front of her, surveyed her nakedness, and grinned a horrible grin. There was no humor in his gap-toothed leer or his hard dark eyes. No humor at all.

Chapter Two

The funky, dark green pickup truck was dirty, dented and dark smoke bulged from the exhaust pipe. It was hardly the expected vehicle of one of Hawaii's most prominent political figures. Dressed in old jeans and a misshapen floppy hat that ensured a "prominent political figure" would go unseen and unrecognized on the streets of Honolulu on this night.

For once, Phillip Greene wasn't in the mode of pandering to the cameras. His advisor, Captain Dodd had requested a covert meeting at a specified and discreet location. Chugging down Diamond Head Road, he passed the old volcano and continued straight on Kahala Avenue through a residential section of nice houses. Dodd had given him specific and detailed instructions on this meeting and, while this was certainly not the quickest or shortest route, it was the most discreet.

Greene hated many people and disliked even more; Dodd however, he feared. While so far Dodd had been polite and almost courteous, there was a coldness about his nature that caused a grip of fear to permeate Greene whenever they met. Dodd exuded a coldness and sense of purpose that indicated he would have "no truck" with anything shorter than complete compliance with his wishes and directions. Greene felt no ambition to test Dodd's limits.

After several switch back turns and false leads as to his direction, Greene eventually came to a stoplight and made a left on Pupukea Road. He drove up the hill and parked off to the side where the road to the Heiau started. He walked about half a block back down Pupukea Road; he had a great view of some of the beaches. He waited there several minutes scanning the road behind him to ensure he wasn't being followed—this was one of several places Dodd had insisted on such a procedure. He walked back to the truck and drove about a mile to the end of the road to the Heiau and parked in the Pu'u o Mahuka Heiau State Monument parking area. Exiting the pickup, he walked about a block on a red dirt trail straight ahead toward the ocean for a nice view of Waimea Bay.

Pu'u o Mahuka Heiau, the largest Heiau or temple complex on the island, covered two acres, its name meaning "Hill of Escape." Legend says it was from this point that Pele, the volcano Goddess, leaped from Oahu to the next island, Molokai. From these commanding heights, sentries could once monitor much of the northern shoreline of Oahu and even spot signal fires from the Wailua complex of Heiaus on the neighboring island of Kauai.

When King Kamehameha conquered Oahu in 1795, his high priest led religious ceremonies there and the Heiau remained in use until the traditional kapu system was abolished in 1819. Kapu was the ancient Code of Conduct; the laws and regulations governed lifestyle, gender roles, politics, religion, etc. The Hawaiian word kapu is usually translated to English as "forbidden," though it also carries the meanings of "sacred," "consecrated," or "holy."

Greene, however was far too sophisticated and urbane to have any relevant feelings for "superstitious crap" such as the kapu. He was there to define his role in the new order, a new order that would place him in permanent power— forever. Greene stood in place for over twenty minutes; he knew he was not alone.

Dodd finally came out of the darkness, "Hello, Mr. Greene. Did you follow my instructions?"

Greene swallowed sharply, the taste of nervous bile building in his throat, "Yes, Captain Dodd, to the letter."

"Excellent," Dodd said. "I am ready to receive your report then." Greene began, starting with the activities of the past weeks.

"I'm pleased to say that my operatives have positioned themselves securely in Michael Rourke's administration and all is going as planned," Greene gushed. "Data is coming in on a daily basis and we have an excellent picture of Rourke's activities."

"What about his father's activities?" Dodd said with a hint of irony in the question. "Michael Rourke is of little consequence to my plan. John Rourke however, is another story."

"John Rourke and his Jew partner Rubenstein are on the Kamchatka Peninsula in an attempt to find Michael's bitch wife, Natalia," Greene said. "Her bogus archeological expedition was intercepted and appears to have been destroyed. I forecast they will find nothing, probably not even her body."

4

"Excellent," Dodd said. "That will obviously occupy their thoughts and actions for some time, reducing the amount of influence they will have on my plans." Suddenly, a voice came out of the darkness on the other side of the clearing.

"Hello Gentlemen, may I join you?"

Dodd's hand flew to the pistol in his left arm pit; his eyes locked on Greene with a killing stare. "Obviously, Mr. Greene, you did not follow my instruction to the letter."

"Actually, Captain Dodd," the voice said, "Mr. Greene did comply exactly with your instructions." The man appeared as a shadow among shadows; removing the black balaclava from his head as he spoke again, "My name is Peter Vale."

Vale was tall, slender and muscular, and spoke with a slight, indiscernible accent. "I believe we are on similar missions. Please Captain, remove your hand from your jacket—empty please. I have no desire to compromise you or your plans; in fact, I would like to place myself and my organization at your disposal. I ask only that you hear me out."

Dodd slowly withdrew his hand. "Gentlemen, I believe we can be allies. Captain Dodd, I hope to convince you that the Neo-Nazi movement could be utilized, if given sufficient encouragement, to create havoc." Dodd listened; havoc was what his Creator was interested in.

"There are a variety of possibilities," Dodd said. "You must understand the short time frame we face. I'm afraid my 'Principal' is interested in a plan with more..." He stopped and thought for a moment then said, "More immediate impact. I believe we will have to add something to the mix in order to acceler- ate our operation." He reached down and picked up the briefcase at his feet and removed a large glass jar with a screw-on lid. "Gentlemen meet our new ally."

Inside the jar was the largest, ugliest insect Greene had ever seen. "A bug? Admittedly a big bug, but it is still just a bug," Greene said.

Greene muttered to the other two men while studying the jar, "I'm not fa- miliar with the species."

Vale smiled, "Nor is anyone else. Mr. Greene, this specimen is capable of moving our agenda further and faster than any political or financial plan. This 'bug' as you call it will make the plagues of Moses pale by comparison."

Chapter Three

Bullets ricocheted in all directions—9mm jacketed hollow point rounds stitched across the driver's side of the silver sports car. Even behind the bullet proof glass and Kevlar panels in the door, Otto Croenberg involuntarily ducked as he swerved violently to the left. Checking the odometer, he was still over a kilometer away from his goal. He reached over to the passenger seat; his bag was still in position. Violently down shifting and jerking the emergency brake, he wrenched the wheel hard to the left—dry skidding down the narrow asphalt drive.

Caught by surprise, the nearest sedan had slammed on its brakes to avoid the collision, fishtailing into the sharp turn. The second sedan flashed through the gap on the right, the driver sending a full magazine of 9mm rounds slamming into the rear windscreen and along the right side of the car. Almost immediately the man realized he had been suckered. Cursing, he dropped the automatic pistol in his lap and tried to compensate. With its brakes squealing and tires smoking, the sedan shot 100 yards past the turn off. By the time he was able to turn around, the sports car and other sedan were out of sight down the drive.

The first sedan tried to regain its lost ground and closed on the sports car; gunfire erupting again from the passenger window. The sports car accelerated away taking advantage of the down slope of the drive; the still waters of the lake less than ten car lengths away. Nanoseconds later it went airborne, flying nearly fifty feet before slamming into the waves and throwing water high into the sky. Landing nose first, it began to sink immediately—seconds before the explosion threw water and flames into the sky. Burning petrol blazed on the waves as the sedan braked and the trailing sedan pulled up alongside.

"Niemand könnte das überleben, no one can survive that," the driver exclaimed.

"Ja, I agree, no one could survive that," the passenger said. "It would be better if we could obtain the body."

"Ja, it would," the driver said. He could hear the sirens of the lake patrol closing on the area. "No time, ve must go."

Chapter Four

Thirty minutes earlier, Otto Croenberg, the soon to be ex-President of the German Republic had been angry... angry, disgusted, and frustrated. His political career, a whirl wind affair, was over. *If I'm not careful* he thought, *so is my life.* Taking the last sip from his coffee cup, he swallowed the now cold and bitter brew, sat the cup down and stood. Looking around the office for the last time, he said to the walls, "Now the specter has raised its ugly head once again." Checking his image in the full length mirror in the corner, he adjusted his tie, picked up the small duffle bag, and strode purposefully out of the office; the door standing open behind him. The clock was ticking on his plan and on his life.

He had ruled Eden City as a quasi, if benevolent, dictator. It had taken several years to accomplish the free election part of his agreement with Rourke. A foundation of his election platform had been for the nationalist aspect of "Rückkehr zum Vaterland," returning to the Fatherland. Since his citizenry identified themselves as German, why not regain their footing on the European continent.

Just over sixty, he had been re-elected to another term; but Croenberg was about to walk out of his New Munich office for the last time. After holding the office of President for the German Republic for three terms and just winning reelection; he had just been derailed. Fifteen minutes earlier, Croenberg had been handed his walking papers—his political career was over. A new Nazi Party's radical agenda, hidden from the public and Croenberg, had just emerged. Once again it was a virulent and hateful aggressive agenda; they had simply been waiting for the "right time." The party leadership had determined that Croenberg's leadership had "moved the German Republic to a position of acceptance and responsibility on the world scene, but that position needed to be consolidated and pushed to the next level."

Almost single handedly, he had been responsible for the relocation of the population from the "old" Eden City from its original location on America's east coast to Europe. Eden City had, at one time, been founded by members of the Eden Project when they returned from their 500 year space mission. They had been called the "last great hope for civilization." Under the leadership of the original Captain Dodd, it had splintered away from American ideals and embraced a nationalistic twist that would manifest itself as a harbinger for Neo-Nazism.

With the help of John Rourke, he had forged a spirit of cooperation and friendship with the American authorities. That had facilitated the move back to Europe, which in turn had allowed the U.S. to regain what had previously been nearly the entire southeast part of America. Over eighty-five percent of the Eden population, slightly over 400,000 souls at that time, agreed to the move—the others swore allegiance to U.S.II.

The move had been accomplished in less than eighteen months. It had allowed a struggling area of the former Fatherland to prosper and it seemed that a new era of positive foreign relations had been forged. In exchange for assistance, control of the eastern American seaboard, and what was left of the Canadian Maritime provinces, was ceded back to U.S.II. Eden City had retained control of the southern tip of Greenland, the few surviving Caribbean nations and northern Brazil. Munich had been chosen as the capital and renamed Eden City.

During the Night of the War, Munich had received little property damage—simply a loss of population due to the neuron "dirty" bombs. It had survived and gradually rebuilt itself. Now, Croenberg realized he must survive and gradually rebuild himself. His citizens had practiced their nationalism in a true and unfettered manner and, for almost twelve years, it had been an unprecedented period of growth and harmony. Through his leadership, the German Republic had been reborn, territory added to the original holdings and now the Republic prospered economically, now boasting almost 1.5 million citizens. It had literally been a win-win-win situation.

In his first meetings with the Rourkes, Otto Croenberg had explored the possibilities of a "temporary" alliance between Croenberg and the Trans-Global Alliance. Croenberg, then in his fifties, was tall and vigorous with gray-blue eyes and a shaven head that occasionally revealed a pulsating vein. At that time, he was also described as a "ruthless and a cold-blooded killer, but only when necessary. No pathological blood lust like say, Karamatsov."

Never one to subscribe to "party propaganda," Croenberg had once agreed there was no proof of racial superiority by any race. He knew there were no differences between whites, Jews, blacks or Chinese, in any basic sense. When John Rourke had offered him the leadership of Eden City itself if he'd forego the Nazi philosophy and agree to free elections in order to stay in power, he accepted.

He had no question that his life was now in jeopardy. One thing the Neo-Nazi movement had in common with its Nazi roots that is neither tolerated opposition. He knew that a dead former President was simply a momentary blip on the news channels. A live former President would be a constant thorn in the sides of his adversaries.

As he walked across the parking garage to his vehicle, he was aware of the bulge in his right sleeve. Otto still carried a small 7.65mm semi-automatic pistol mounted to a muscle-group activated slide mechanism on his right arm; he was never without that backup piece. While his primary language was German, his English was quite good; and though normally accented, it could be perfect when the need arose and he was adept at disguise. He knew he must disappear and decided he had less than eight hours to effect that disappearance and plug the hole so he would not be sought after. It was time to commit suicide and he was ready.

He laid the small duffle bag on the passenger seat and undid the top and opened it; the quick scan told him everything was still in place. He had started this plan three years ago when he first suspected that the Progressives within the party were positioning themselves for the move they had just completed. But, he knew it was essential to his survival to re-establish contact with the Rourke family, even though Michael Rourke had once described him also as "evil." He had once told Michael, "I have always believed that the true test of genius is the ability to take advantage of opportunity, then capitalize on the present rather than vainly plan for a future which may never come." When he finally met John Rourke, a sort of truce between Croenberg and the Rourkes had begun.

He felt Paul Rubenstein was the linchpin to his plan. His relationship with Paul Rubenstein, who he had simply referred to as "the Jew" in those early days, had changed during their shared adventures. Paul had called Otto, "the Nazi" but a begrudging friendship had slowly been forged, with "the Jew" becoming "Herr Rubenstein." He had a bond with the Rourkes and it was likely they were his only salvation; provided he survived his suicide.

Snapping his seat belt, he glanced in his rear view mirror and spotted the two black sedans. As he pulled out of the garage they followed him. *Hmmm,* he thought. *The game is already afoot.* The tinted windscreen prevented him from identifying the vehicles' occupants but he knew they were a hit squad. He focused on his immediate situation. His route would carry him through Munich and into the countryside. *That will be where the attack will happen,* he thought to himself.

His primary questions were simple. *Can I survive the attacks?* he thought. *Can I make it to my target in time and intact enough to commit suicide ... correctly?*

Chapter Five

There were still several kilometers left to get to the Fünfseenland; from the running gun battle, it might has well have been several hundred. Of the five lakes in the Fünfseenland, Starnberger was the second largest lake in Bavaria at 20 kilometers long, 5 kilometers wide and up to 127 meters deep. It was bordered by moraine hills with higher mountains of Benediktenwand and the Wetterstein mountain range in the background. He could have reached it via the subterranean train, but that would not allow him to implement phase two of his plan.

Starnberger, like Ammersee, Wörthsee, Pilsensee and Wesslinger Lakes had been formed by ice-age glaciers. The alpine panorama of the Starnberger Sea offered an unforgettable sight, with numerous meadows and beaches, perfect for relaxation and enjoying one's self; his focus however, was not on relaxation or enjoyment... it was survival. He had picked the details of his plan with cold calculation; he would have only one chance... and it wasn't much of a chance to live. He watched the two sedans make their move, closing the distance. *It won't be long now*, he thought.

Moments later, Croenberg's car plowed through the rail at over seventy kilometers per hour, sailed over fifty yards in a down sloped arch and exploded shortly after impact. Otto Croenberg, former president of the German Republic, died in a flash of thunder—the chilling cold waters of the lake swallowing what was left of his mangled vehicle.

Chapter Six

The analysis of the recovered UFO found at the Waiāhole Ditch and Tunnel System, piloted by Captain Dodd during the attack on Honolulu, was not going well. Technicians at Hickam Air Force Base were stumped. Once access had been gained to the interior of the craft, they discovered that the cabin was small by aircraft standards. It was as if the pilot had to "wear" the craft to fly it. The pilot's "chair" was on a locking swivel; the pilot would enter the craft, sit down then spin the chair ninety degrees and lock the seat. The place where the control panel should sit was blank, no dials and no gauges, just two panels located on either side.

General Francis Sullivan, Deputy Air Force Chief of Staff, shook his head. Looking to his left he asked, "Well Colonel, we know this thing flies... can you figure out how to fly it?"

Colonel Rodney Thorne, chief flight instructor and test pilot, turned to the senior Flight Surgeon, "All I have is a hypothesis. I can't find any physical interface between the pilot and the craft in the conventional concept. I think there must be either a direct or indirect connection between the pilot's brain and the craft. I don't see any other way to maneuver the craft during the flight characteristics we have witnessed."

"I tend to agree with the Colonel's analysis," Dr. B.J. Dalton, senior Flight Surgeon said to the Air Force Chief of Staff. "Sensory areas receive and process information that is interpreted by the brain and the brain tells the body what to do and how to do it. I think in this process the cerebral cortex is tapped and controls the craft; I'm not sure how you would actually classify the process. Telepathy is a possibility but I suspect it is actually a mix of mechanical and possibly some sort of paranormal connection or conduit. It is probable we have some similar technology but there is obviously a part missing from this equa- tion. Possibly there is a helmet we haven't discovered, I don't know, but there has to be some method of making the connection between the pilot's brain and the craft. I just don't know what that method is."

Mid-Wake's senior metallurgist, Isaac Johnson joined the discussion. "I'm afraid I can't add much to this discussion. I do not have a clue what this thing is made of. I can tell you it did not roll off the assembly line at General Motors. The samples we recovered from the crash sites of the other UFOs during air battle above Honolulu do not resemble anything on our Periodic Tables. Whatever this material is, it did not come from Earth." Johnson leaned back in his chair. "Sorry guys, I just don't know what to tell you."

The Chief of Staff asked, "Colonel, do you think you can fly this thing?"

Horne rubbed his chin, "Can it be flown? Yes. Could I fly it? Probably. The problem is one of the super brains is going to have to tell me how to turn the damn thing on and take off. Frankly, I don't have a clue."

"Wait a minute," Dalton said and started thumbing through a stack of files. "Here it is. This is a report of an incident involving Captain Dodd's clone that was captured during the Fight in the Forest and Akiro Kuriname who was captured after the recent incident with President Michael Rourke. When Dodd died unexpectedly while being interrogated, John Rourke thought there might be some connection between a tattoo Dodd had and his death. When Kuriname was captured after the attack on the President, John Rourke surgically—and that term is only loosely accurate—removed a similar tattoo from him. Kuriname survived and is doing well. Could the connection between the pilot and the ship be the tattoo?"

Heads shook around the table, Johnson said, "Hell if I know. I could speculate and say yes but I have no idea how it would work."

Colonel Horne said after a moment, "That technology exceeds anything we are familiar with. Hypothetically, why not? That might be the answer. However, if it is, the ship will not fly again. I'm not willing to subject myself to an alien mind link in the interest of national security." Thorn took a sip of black coffee, "Look, flight is flight regardless of the technology and avionics. This craft has superior capabilities but that does not make it a super weapon, just a superior one. I believe these capabilities are finite; extreme by our sciences but not infinite."

"I suggest you get to work on how to turn it on. Get it turned on and I'll figure out how to control this thing and make it fly. We don't have anything in our arsenal that has its flight characteristics or weapons capabilities. One ship may not be enough to stop an invasion but it could be a hell of a surprise for the invaders. It could buy us a little time."

Chapter Seven

Croenberg unbuckled his seatbelt and grabbed the bag next to him, wrapping a tether cord around his left wrist. Opening the vehicle console he pulled the small underwater rebreather pack, slipped on the dive mask and tightly gripped the mouth piece with his teeth. Attached to the rebreather was a small transmitter; Croenberg flipped the switch from standby to armed.

As he came up on his target, he swerved slightly to get the maximum lift from the slight rise at the water line. He flipped the switch a second time and aimed for the split rail fence. The impact of the water jarred his senses as he dove out of the car door and swam for his life—straight down. The car was less than half submerged when it detonated. With his hands over his ears, he rode out the concussive wave that slammed into him. The Kevlar padding within his suit coat dispersed most of the shook wave and kept the concussion from scrambling his internal organs; he tasted blood as he dove deeper still before leveling out.

Shedding his suit coat and shoes, he began the mile-long underwater swim. The near freezing waters of the lake made it difficult but his closed circuit rebreather unit worked as required, producing no tell-tell bubbles on the surface. Fifteen minutes later he surfaced, got his bearings, and submerged again; the CCR gauge showed almost two hours of oxygen remaining in the small cylinder. Strong kicks and powerful strokes propelled him underwater toward the backside of Roseninsel, the only island in the lake. Rising slowly, he gently broke the surface; with his face still half submerged he scanned the beach—empty.

Roseninsel, or Rose Island, had been the site of a royal villa of King Ludwig II of Bavaria. In the mid-1800s, his father Maximilian had started the project but died before its completion. Ludwig, fond of the island, had hosted Richard Wagner, Prince Paul of Thurn, an Austrian empress, and a Russian Czarina there. The villa was been transformed into a small museum, open to the general public, but that was before the Night of the War. Now the island was deserted except for the occasional fisherman or young couple looking for an au natural sexual experience.

Stiff and shivering from the cold, he crawled all of the way to shore, careful not to show a silhouette against his surroundings; he spat out the mouth piece. After catching his breath, he removed ankle-high hiking boots from his water-tight bag and stowed the rebreather before heading inland. With a total land mass of just under five acres, he didn't have far to go but the going wasn't easy. Gone were the formal gardens that had given the island its name; in their place grew wild vines with almost quarter-inch stickers. By the time he reached his goal, what remained of his pant legs were ripped by the vicious thorns; blood ran from lacerations on his forearms and dripped from his fingers.

Peering through the brush, he could see the flashing lights of the rescue boats in the distance and the small helicopter circling the crash site looking for his body. *So far, so good,* he thought.

Chapter Eight

Göbekli Tepe, Turkey:

Natalia knew what was coming next—rape. Her feet were untied, her hands now secured in front of her naked body. Her attacker jerked her to a standing position. He leered and his eyes bore into hers. Glancing over his shoulder he nodded his head in the direction of the tent; his leer came back and she knew that would be the scene of her debauchery. Slumping her shoulders she looked at the ground; she hoped her signs of submission would be taken for resignation. If the bastard bought that she had resigned herself to his attention, it might give her the chance that she needed. She mentally measured the distance to her target—the neck of a broken bottle on the ground.

The Mongol pulled the tent cover back and shoved her inside. She fell on the floor of the tent, grabbed the broken bottle and hid it between her palms; she whimpered. *So far, so good*, she thought, *not much of a weapon but still a weapon*. The Mongol jerked off the heavy coat and undid his trousers. His guttural speech was indecipherable but his intent was plain. He pulled a wicked dagger as his pants dropped and held it point up under Natalia's throat; again she whimpered, louder this time.

Using the rope as a leash, he positioned her on her back and stabbed the knife into the ground next to her head. *Here it comes*, she thought as the filthy bastard dropped on top of her. She squirmed and the Mongol slapped her, hard; her head swam and her vision blurred for a moment. Going limp seemed the best way to get the advantage so she relaxed. The Mongol was on his knees between her thighs ready to penetrate her; he leaned down and that was when Natalia struck.

Her hands still lashed together with the bottle neck nestled inside them; she viciously whipped the broken bottle neck up burying two inches of it in the man's Adam's apple before jerking it out through the right side of his neck, severing the carotid artery. She wrapped her legs around his body, pulling his head down; she held on for dear life as he struggled. With his windpipe and voice box destroyed, the only sounds that escaped could be mistaken as sounds of passion. After a minute, his struggles grew noticeably weaker; another minute passed, the man had bled out and was still.

Natalia roughly shoved the man's body off of her. The left side of her body was now sticky with his blood from half way up her arm to her shoulder; her back was covered with it. Her attack had been perfect and her results what she had expected. *Now what?* She thought as she allowed her breathing to return to normal. Periodically, she moaned loudly so the others would believe the rape was still going on. She grabbed the dagger and cut the rope binding her hands. She grabbed the bottle of water on the desk and washed the blood from her body and pulled on her clothes; the first she had worn in hours.

Quietly searching the tent, she found her Bali-Song knife and her back up pistol, a Model 39 Smith and Wesson, and three magazines. The Smith had a single stack magazine which meant she only had nine rounds available before she had to reload. *It will have to do for now*, she decided. *Better than nothing.* Moving to the corner of the tent she found what she was hoping for, a guitar case. Unzipping the case she pulled out a CAR 15 and an MP-5 from their custom cutout slots in the Styrofoam, and three 30-round magazines for each weapon.

She took a deep breath. *Ok*, she thought, *I'm on foot, miles from help in a camp full of crazies—shit.* Taking a deep breath, she placed a magazine in each weapon, stowing the spares in her coat's cargo pockets. She jerked the charging handles, loaded a round in the chamber of both rifles and flipped the selector switches to full auto. *Now,* she thought, *I'm as ready as I'm going to get.*

Pulling the tent flap slightly open she glanced outside and then she moved. The camp was still asleep. *I might actually be able to make it out of here.* She didn't see one of the Mongols walk around the edge of the tent behind her—but he saw her.

Chapter Nine

Kamchatka Peninsula:

The attack lasted only fifteen minutes but it had been fifteen minutes of hell. While the attack had been a total surprise, Sanderson's insertion team reacted quickly and effectively. The only good news was the Russian attackers, while well placed before they attacked, was a small force and they had underestimated their opponents.

Four of Sanderson's insertion team had died almost immediately, caught in the initial cross fire. Six others, including Paul Rubenstein, had non-life threatening injuries. Eight of the attackers had survived, including one that had caught Sanderson's attention. The boy was a local, dressed in garb that Sanderson recognized. Sanderson pulled the young man out of the circle of Russians being interrogated. They walked away from the group; Sanderson motioned for his captive to sit.

A look of surprise jolted the captive's face; Sanderson was speaking to him in his own language. Though it was a different regional dialect, they could communicate. "How do you know my tongue?" he said.

"Because I am one of the people," Sanderson said quietly and handed the man a cigarette. Lighting it he asked, "Why are you with these people?"

"How do I know you're one of the people? You may have just learned our language."

Sanderson thought and reached inside his uniform blouse, pulling out the bone carving. "Long ago my father gave this to me. My village was wiped out and I went to live with these people. Satisfied?"

The captive studied the horse carving and nodded. "I had no choice; they came to our village three days ago and took me. They promised they would let me go after I guided them here to you, but I did not believe them. I have heard stories about some of our people who left. I always thought they were just stories though."

"Are there more of them?" Sanderson asked.

The captive shook his head, "I don't think so, I never saw any others. They came from the sky in one of those flying machines with whirling blades on their top."

Sanderson nodded but kept his expression blank, *A helicopter, there's a piece of luck.* "How far is your village?"

"Two valleys over," the captive said. "At least what is left of it. I saw them kill many and burn many yurts. I don't know who or what is left of it."

Sanderson stood and motioned for Rourke to come over. Rourke was tending to the three wounded, he patted Rubenstein's shoulder and said, "Paul give me a minute. I'll be right back," then walked toward Sanderson. "What do you need Wes?"

"Got something John, this guy is one of my people. Three days ago a chopper landed in his village and these guys took him prisoner and made him guide them to us."

"A chopper, huh," Rourke said with a smile.

"Yep," Sanderson said, returning the smile.

"That's lucky."

"More than you know John. Our radio and communication equipment were knocked out in that attack."

"No one back home got our distress call?" Rourke asked.

Sanderson shook his head, "Don't think so but I can't be sure. Sparks just tried to get a message out but the radio and satellite equipment is fried."

"How far away is the village?"

"Two valleys over," Sanderson said. "At least what is left of it. This one saw several people being killed and yurts burning."

Rourke nodded and thought for a moment. "Then we need to head toward that village. If the chopper is still there we can make contact with our own folks and have the injured evacuated and our prisoners turned over for interrogation."

Several shots rang out behind him and Rourke spun dropping to one knee, the Detonics from under his left arm at full extension.

"We are under orders John to take no prisoners," Sanderson said, as his operators executed the remaining wounded Mongols.

Rourke nodded, stood and reholstered the .45 nodded saying, "Then let's get our wounded out of here."

Chapter Ten

Göbekli Tepe, Turkey:

She never saw her attacker but, in the last second, she heard the swish of the blow driving toward her head; she twisted. That slight turn of her head kept the impact of the pummel of his heavy sword from crushing her skull. The glancing force of the blow was enough to stun her; pain and darkness swirled around her as she dropped to one knee. Both rifles went skidding across the dirt, unfired. Body odor and the foul smell of airag—the fermented mare's milk that passed for Mongol alcohol—assailed her sense of smell as she was jerked to her feet. She was thrown through the air landing back inside the tent.

Her attacker leaned down to pick her up again; she slashed the Bali-Song in a sweeping arch, transecting his trachea and carotid arteries in one sweep. The crash of his body slamming into the storage locker contained in the tent was the only noise he made. But it was enough to bring a second attacker.

Rising to one knee she slashed again, lower this time, severing the muscles of the second man's stomach and dumping his intestines on the floor of the tent. There was just enough time for one thrust before her head and neck slammed into the edge of the table; she was unconscious. Her last thought had been a vague awareness of the sound of an engine. The filthy Mongol lay on top of her—dead, while Natalia lay there slowly bleeding out from her own wounds—dying. The sounds of the engine were gone.

Chapter Eleven

Kamchatka Peninsula:

Rourke saw the aircraft first and pointed to the sky, "Are those ours or Russian?"

Sanderson strained his eyes, "Looks like they are ours, they should be the combat air patrol planes. If they're ours they'll start a circular pattern overhead. If they circle, they're protecting us with a combat air patrol protocol and the transporters should be here shortly to evacuate us. If they don't—we're toast; that'll mean they're Russian and we're going to get hammered."

Rourke walked over to Paul, putting his hand on his shoulder. "How's the leg?" Paul had taken a taken a hit in his right leg; while painful, it wasn't life threatening.

"Hurts but I've had worse. Those planes are ours I hope."

Both watched—neither sure if the approaching planes were their salvation or their ruin. Rourke smiled, "They are starting the circle pattern, they're ours," he shouted to Sanderson.

"Won't be long now then," Sanderson hollered back after he scanned the skies himself.

Thirty minutes later, the wounded had been loaded and two giant jet powered vertical takeoff and landing transports, or VTOLs, were lifting up. The crew chief came back to Rourke, "Aircraft Commander wants to see you upfront, Sir."

Rourke unbuckled his seat restraint and stepped over Rubenstein's stretcher, secured on the deck at his feet. "Back in a minute, Paul," Rourke said and went forward. He climbed up the access ladder to the flight deck and knocked. Someone flipped the latch and pushed the door open, "Come in Sir." The flight engineer sat back down at his console and handed Rourke a headset with a boom microphone and flipped a switch on his console.

"Do I call you Doctor, General or what Sir?" the pilot said, turning slightly in his seat to face Rourke.

"How about, John, Major," Rourke said.

"Roger that John, need you to listen to something. Play it for him Sparks." Rourke, holding one earphone to his head heard a garbled message that ended in mid-sentence. He frowned, "When did you get this Major?"

"Mid-Wake got it yesterday over the satellites. We're headed there now."

"Does the President know?" Rourke asked.

"Yes Sir," the pilot said. "Would you like to speak with him directly?"

Rourke took a deep breath, wiped his face with one hand then nodded. The pilot keyed his radio, "Rescue, Rescue this is Alpha 357."

"Go ahead Alpha 357."

"Do you have that connection ready? The other party is standing by."

"Roger, 357. Connecting now."

"No names or titles Sir, the bad guys may be listening." Rourke nodded and slid the headphone into position and held the microphone switch in his left hand.

"Are you there? Over." Rourke recognized the voice immediately. It was his son Michael.

"I am, go ahead. Over."

"I am rerouting you to another location, your pilot will explain. The Göbekli Tepe project has been attacked. There has been no further contact and I don't know what you will be walking into but you're the closest help available. You know what is at stake there? Over."

Rourke took a deep breath and let it out slowly before answering. "Affirmative, I'll find her. Over." He had heard the anguish in his son's voice.

"I have a follow up force coming to assist you, but it will not arrive until after you have made contact. What you have with you is what you have, but you do have the air support from the combat air control with you; do you copy? Over."

"Affirmative, I'll advise you as soon as I can. Over."

"Tango, Yankee, Delta. Out." Michael had spelled out the first letters for Thank You Dad.

"Yankee, Whiskey, Sierra. Out." *You're welcome Son.* The connection was broken and Rourke grasped the pilot's shoulder. "How long before we get there?"

The pilot looked at his watch and answered, "You've got about an hour and a half at this speed. Check with the crew chief, we brought a resupply of ammo for you. Here is what we know right now," he handed Rourke a printout. Rourke scanned the printout quickly, "This says a transport plane is enroute to rendezvous with us.

"Yes, Sir and it is on schedule. I'll give you a fifteen minute heads up before we land." Rourke slapped him on the shoulder, stripped the headphone and headed out.

Rourke spotted Sanderson and waved for him to come. Stepping through the maze of stretchers on the deck, Sanderson asked, "What is it John?"

"We have a problem," Rourke said. "How many of the men can still fight?"

"Four dead, six wounded; that leaves fourteen counting you and me," Sanderson said. "Two of the wounded are relatively minor; we could use them if we had to. What's going on?" Sanderson listened as Rourke briefed him. He checked his watch and said, "We're less than an hour and a half out; excuse me, I have things to do," Sanderson said as he turned. Rourke went to Rubenstein and briefed him.

Chapter Twelve

Near Göbekli Tepe, Turkey:

The VTOL transports landed about three miles from the encampment and off loaded the special operations team. Rourke watched as the transport approached from the west; the rear ramp opened and discharged something— several chutes deployed. Through his binoculars Rourke saw a speck; it was a man in free fall. Suddenly, he spread his arms and legs, flying horizontally instead of falling. *Wing suit,* Rourke thought. *This should be interesting.*

The lone jumper dove to catch up with the other chutes. The cargo and the jumper floated gently to less than 100 yards from the team; Sanderson and six of his men jogged to the landing site. As Sanderson and his men detached the chutes, Rourke could now see they were vehicles but unlike any he was familiar with. Engines cranked and the vehicles headed back with drivers; it looked like the jumper was riding with Sanderson.

The strange vehicles parked in a row; Sanderson's passenger approached on foot, "You Dr. Rourke?"

John nodded at the man while he stripped the wing suit off. A battle dress uniform came into view; a Colonel's eagle insignia on each collar. "General Sullivan has stood up a new Joint Commando Brigade, Dr. Rourke. My name is Colonel John Ball, friends call me Jack. Sullivan ordered me here to help in this mission. I've spoken with Chief Sanderson and he and I are good. Hope this won't be a problem for you."

Rourke shook his head, "If Wes doesn't have a problem I don't either. But you need to understand, we're here to rescue my daughter-in-law. That is my only concern; do anything... anything at all to jeopardize that..." Rourke let the sentence fall off as he pulled his battered Zippo and a thin dark cigar from his pocket. Once it was going to his satisfaction he looked back at Ball. "Do anything to jeopardize this mission and you and I will have a problem. Understood?"

Ball stood quietly under Rourke's gaze and lighted cigar. "I'm here to help Sir. We're on the same side."

Rourke nodded and looked over at the strange vehicles. "Then call me John and tell me, what the hell are those things?"

Ball smiled, "It is a new breed of what is an All Terrain Powered Armored Attack Vehicle. This ATPAAV is called the Griffin, after the winged lion of Greek mythology. In addition to negotiating rough terrain, it has limited flight capabilities. It combines an all-terrain dune buggy with a 'micro-light' aircraft. It is designed to take off and fly in powered flight or paraglide."

"The AATVs you're familiar with were the last generation and while extremely serviceable had some drawbacks. The main ones being it was only lightly armored and totally terrestrial. These Griffins are intended to deploy on a range of missions from hostage rescue and reconnaissance, to equipment transport and difficult to reach targets that require air drop."

Rourke watched as parasails were attached to hook-up points at the top of the roof and stretched out behind the Griffins. "So what can they do?"

Ball led Rourke to the nearest Griffin, the one that Wes Sanderson was working on. Ball looked skyward as he gathered his thoughts. He began to explain, "It's a hybrid combining a dune buggy with an ultra-light aircraft with a ceiling of more than 10,000 feet. It has STOL, Short Take Off and Landing capabilities, meaning it requires less than 330 feet to take off and can land in under 33 feet—even on poorly prepared fields. It can carry either one or two people and can stay in the air up to three hours. In the air, it can travel at speeds between 35 to 50 miles per hour."

"On the land, depending on the terrain, it can reach up to about 65 mph and manage both dry and wet obstacles. It's designed to provide access to tough spots—overcoming rivers, dunes, cliffs, damaged roads and more. The vehicle's silent propellers ensure a stealth approach. In addition to the crew, it can carry up to approximately 550 pounds of cargo to include weapons ranging from machine guns to light multi-role missiles."

"These use regular gasoline for fuel, but later evolutions will most likely use the more readily available downrange diesel fuel. The passenger seat can be removed to provide space for combat kits like weapons or equipment. Compact and light, the Griffin is air-transportable and, can be deployed from aircraft like these or driven off during flight without the plane having to land. This is a key advantage because it can make rapid access to hard-to-reach places a whole lot easier."

"In addition to rapid deployment, it has also been designed to provide a speedy yet quiet approach to support fast intervention on the ground. Beyond combat applications, the vehicle could also be used for civil security as well as non-governmental organizations' responses to natural disasters and humanitarian crises. Hell, it could even be used for tourism."

Rourke walked around and sat down in the driver's compartment. Turning to Sanderson, he asked, "You familiar with these?"

"Yes," Sanderson said. "During the test trials with the military, December of last year, we were trained on them. John, I'll tell you they are pretty remarkable little toys. And there are different types."

"More than one version?" Rourke asked.

"Yes and no," Sanderson explained. The same frame is used in all but there are different modules that change from mission to mission. All ATPAAVs are powered by a 125 horsepower one-liter turbocharged three-cylinder engine, but they can be fitted with several module configurations. The Max is the plain Jane ATPAAV, ones that don't fly. They are very robust and agile; all terrain tactical vehicles that reach up to about 60 miles per hour on the highway and can carry a payload of up to 1,500 pounds."

"The second is the Viking, that module is a snow mobile conversion kit. The front tires are replaced with steerable skids, while heavy lugged rear tires with ice spikes provide thrust in snow or over ice. There is a conversion for underwater work called Nautilus. It is for SCUBA depths only and within normal SCUBA operational envelopes. The Griffin, the flying model, operates on the same flight characteristics as an ultra-light or powered parasail. The cost is only about $100,000 for a single ATPAAV, with each module costing an addition $10,000 to $30,000 bucks. Good news is we won't have to walk to the target and they'll never hear us coming."

"And the better news is we can make an aerial pass over on the target, without alerting the bad guys and get Intel that will help us when we move out,"

Sanderson said. "We have configured five of them to carry our assault troops. One is fitted with twin .30 caliber machine guns and the last has been stripped to the frame to haul wounded out of the area."

Rourke nudged Sanderson who called over another trooper to finish modifications on the Griffin. Rourke said, "Let's talk." They walked off several yards so they couldn't be overheard. Rourke finally stopped and pulled another cigar and lit it for Sanderson, "What do you know about Ball?"

Chapter Thirteen

"He presented his orders to me and they're legit," Sanderson said to Rourke. "The new Joint Commando Brigade was created by General Sullivan. It is comprised of Lieutenant Commander Kuriname's men, my Special Forces Operators, and Marine Air and Naval Transport teams. Colonel Ball is the commander. They will operate directly under Sullivan's orders and those orders will come directly from the President. His nickname is 'Mad Jack.' Frankly John, in the SpecOps community, he's a bit of a legend."

"Tell me about it," John said

"Several years ago," Sanderson began, "there was an assault against a Neo-Nazi garrison on the coast of South America. The first thing the Nazi garrison heard was the sudden blaring drone of bagpipes. One commando stood at the front of the landing craft, facing the impending battle and playing the peppy martial, 'March of the Cameron Men.' The landing craft came to rest on shore and that soldier jumped from the craft and chunked a grenade before drawing a full sword, screaming, running into the fray."

"Colonel Ball has gained a reputation for his 'stunts,' and this was hardly the first or most bizarre and semi-suicidal of his life. 'Mad Jack,' as he is known, is battle hardened. During several ongoing conflicts he has survived multiple explosions, escaped capture several times, and captured more than forty prisoners at sword point—in just one raid. He also scored the last recorded longbow kill in history."

"Within the Special Operations community, not to mention arm chair war junkies and badass aficionados, Mad Jack's exploits have become the epitome of military romanticism. While a professional warrior of the highest degree, he also has swagger. In civilian media accounts, he is known for two of his most publicized comments: 'Any officer who goes into action without his sword is improperly dressed,' and 'I maintain that, as long as you tell a German loudly and clearly what to do, if you are senior to him he will cry 'Jawohl' and get on with it enthusiastically and efficiently.'"

"British by ancestry, he graduated from military academy and, at age twenty, was shipped off to fight; unfortunately at a time where fighting was nonexistent. Bored by a long period of inactivity, Ball left the military and spent some time as a newspaper editor, male model, and as a bagpipe-playing, arrow-shooting extra in several low-budget movies. By the end of the decade, he'd become so obsessed with the pipes that he took second place in a piping competition—causing a mild scandal because he was the first non-Scot to accomplish this feat. The next year, his archery expertise landed him a place as a shooter at the World Archery Championship."

"As things began to heat back up and battles with the brigand hoards that still populated parts of North America became imminent, Ball rushed back to the battlefield, along with his longbow. His skills in guerilla tactics and staging raids earned him several commendations for bravery, even surviving a clipping by machine gunfire. Once, while watching a brigand force advance from a tower in a small village, Ball signaled the attack by shooting the leader of the brigand band through the chest with a barbed arrow, immediately followed by a hail of bullets from two fellow infantrymen in tow."

"The next year, Ball volunteered to join the newly formed Special Operations team. In the next conflict he launched another raid. Surviving the battle unscathed, a demolition 'expert' had accidentally detonated a charge next to him, sending shards from the bottle of whiskey he was drinking into his forehead. Following a short rehabilitation, he was back on his feet soon after, joining the next campaign."

"On another raid, he and a corporal crept from one enclosure to the next, surprising the guards with his claymore sword. By the end of the night, he'd captured forty-two prisoners with a sword and soon after earned the Distinguished Service Cross."

"Once, in a joint operation with Wolfgang Mann's forces, Ball led a full frontal assault on a well-defended force. Leading a charge through strafing fire and mortars, he was one of only seven men to reach the target; and, after firing off every bullet he had, found himself the last man standing. So he stood playing 'Will Ye No Come Back Again?' on his pipes until the advancing Neo Nazis knocked him out with a grenade blast. The Nazis reportedly ignored orders to kill him out of respect."

"After proving he had no valuable Intel and causing panic by lighting a trash fire during one of his moves, he escaped the camp, shimmying under a wire fence, and attempted to walk back to his own team. Captured just miles from the friendly forces, he was transferred to another camp. He escaped, sneaking away during a power outage and walking for three days, using a stolen rusted can to cook what he considered 'liberated' chickens and vegetables until he found the Allied regiment and convinced them he was a 'friendly.'"

"While his equipment might have seemed outdated, it did serve its purpose on the battlefield. 'Both the longbow and the claymore were extremely effective in the right circumstances,' one weapons historian said. 'Both are capable of maiming and killing.' Based on images of Ball, the historian suspected he used a lightweight bow with a draw weight under 40 pounds, versus the 100-pound medieval bows and 180-pound modern war bows. It seemed that unarmored troops presented a softer target than men in armor during the middle ages. Consequently, a really heavy bow would not be necessary."

"Modern bow hunters say a 70-pound draw bow can drop a deer easily at 20 yards, and a 40-pound bow would have a greater range, with lesser impact, so its killing potential in early modern times was still notable. Plus the bow had the benefit of silent firing."

"Ball didn't use his bow for stealth warfare, though. This was a man known to charge enemies waving a sword and screaming 'Take 'em Boys!' at the top of his lungs. This sort of bravado might have been a tactic used to intimidate the enemy into fearing the charge of an unexpected madman. But that tactical pomp and ceremony had limited utility, and wearing a sword could bog one down in landings and hamper movement through tight presses of men."

"Infantry warfare entails a lot of crawling on your belly and maneuvering into ambush positions. The clatter and clutter of a sword would not be helpful in such situations. That is why the historian referred to Ball's advocacy of the sword in modern battle as 'Romantic affectation.'"

"Recognizing Ball's bravery," Sanderson continued, "his survival may have had just as much to do with his assumed insanity as it did with his skill and true grit. A Scottish piper had played the pipes on the beaches of Normandy. German soldiers had seen him on the beaches but didn't fire because they thought he was obviously crazy. Similarly, there may be as much pity and confusion as intimidation and fear on the other side of the stories of Mad Jack."

"A glimpse into Ball's psyche suggests his madness wasn't all fun story fodder worthy of lionization. Shooting someone with a longbow as the overture to opening up with rifles doesn't suggest a specific advantage for using the longbow in that situation. Personally, I think it was of a macabre curiosity he had about killing someone with a longbow. If there was a glint of psychopathy in Ball, he kept a tight lid on it."

Sanderson walked off leaving Rourke thoroughly fascinated and a little apprehensive.

Chapter Fourteen

Gunnery Sergeant Ferguson could walk, though not well or for any distance. He had made it perfectly clear, "I'm not going to be left behind." Barely ambulatory, he could drive, shoot and work communications which would be essential if they had a chance to save Natalia. Once in position Rourke and Sanderson would take the remaining force, a total of 16 men, and move on the encampment. Gunny Ferguson had experience as a FAC, Forward Air Controller, and could communicate with the jets above for close air support during the raid. With hostile targets that close to Sanderson and Rourke's teams, the fighter jets would have to "thread the needle" with GPS guided ordnance to keep from killing the "friendlies." The Gunny could only use one hand and his right leg.

The Griffins had silently landed on the opposite side of the nearest hill; once their parasails had been dropped they were ready for the assault. Colonel Ball had made a high level pass to survey the campsite and radioed, "Looks like they're still asleep. Several tents but only one seems to be guarded. Ready when you are."

Rourke and his seven men approached the encampment from the west and Sanderson with his seven were driving hard from the west/northwest. The plan was to drive the Mongols southwestward down toward the steppe away from the camp. If successful, they would flee downhill away from the threat of attack. That attack had to be swift and decisive enough to either drive them off or kill them all, almost immediately.

Rourke knew that would be the easy part. The hard part would be trying to find Natalia... or what was left of her. Rourke shook his head to drive out the thoughts. Paul grasped Rourke's shoulder, "She'll be fine, John. You know how tough she is." Rourke just nodded as he parked the ATPAAV below the crest of a hill and formed up his team. Rourke checked his Rolex Submariner and nodded to Rubenstein who keyed his radio, sending out a single short transmission that "squawked" the airways. He listened and received two short squawks back. He nodded to Rourke; Sanderson was in place and starting his attack. Rourke moved his people out.

Gunfire erupted as Sanderson's team blasted down the hill. High above, Mad Jack Ball dove his Griffin and approached the camp from behind a hill. He would make the first pass with the twin machine guns mounted on the Griffin's front fenders. That would be followed by one of the three jets that had pulled out of formation with the Combat Air Patrol and was diving. Screaming down out of the clear blue sky, Ferguson directed the pilot to send two smart rockets down just short of the camp, between it and the attacking force under Sanderson, with less than 200 yards to spare. Mad Jack strafed the area closest to the tents.

The plan worked like a charm, scattering most of the enemy away from the camp. There was no way to know if any of the hostages were still alive. The plan was to confuse the enemy and drive them away, hoping in the process they wouldn't stand and fight; or even worse, take the time to kill any of the hostages—if there were any left.

Mad Jack pushed the throttle forward and accelerated, climbing for another run at the camp as the missiles from the jet destroyed Mongols. Suddenly, his motor sputtered and vibrations began to violently shake the Griffin. Glancing behind him, he noticed that one of the rotor blades were missing. "Shit," he shouted to the sky and pulled on the toggle handle and swung the Griffin into a dive. He had to land before he crashed.

The smart rockets, guided by GPS coordinates, impacted perfectly in the "eye of the needle." The encampment was below the crest of the hill on which Gunny Ferguson sat. Slinging his useless left leg out of the way, he stood and grasped the machine gun mounted on the crash bar above the passenger seat as he pulled himself erect. He flipped the safety off, jerked the charging handle, and directed his fire just to the north of the encampment.

Some of the Mongols burst from the tents, while others having passed out on the ground sprang into action and started returning fire. Ferguson swung the heavy machine gun to the right and sprayed those farthest from the tents. Rourke, Rubenstein and the rest of his team drove hard from the left flank. One Mongol hollered something and stood, spraying rounds at Rourke's team. He was cut down immediately. Several others broke out running toward their horses; about twenty of the bandits made it, galloping off down the hill leaving their companions to face death.

The pilot had pulled a lot of Gs pulling up his jet and banking hard over. On his second pass, an additional rocket and a spray of 20mm cannon reduced more of the Mongols to bits and pieces of horse and human body parts, exploding under the barrage. Sanderson and his six-man team made the encampment first and the battle quickly degenerated into hand-to-hand combat with knives and side-arms.

Chapter Fifteen

Ball's Griffin slammed into the ground harder than he wanted, the impact temporarily stunning him. Slowly he hit the release on his harness and fell out of the Griffin. He stumbled to the rear and saw the stub of the missed blade—there was half a bullet hole. A slug had pierced the blade and the stress of the climb had broken off the rest of it. He heard hoofbeats behind him and turned to see a lone Mongol galloping toward him.

Jerking his mount to a halt, the Mongol sat in the saddle with his rifle trained on Ball. He pointed at the rifle then pointed to the sky and smiled. He had scored the hit on Mad Jack's Griffin. Mad Jack bowed from the waist and smiled back; one warrior acknowledging the accomplishment of a worthy enemy. The Mongol nodded, dropped the sling of the rifle over the saddle horn, and dismounted.

He pulled the wicked curved bladed sword and smiled again; Mad Jack recognized a challenge when he saw one and grinned. He slowly drew his side-arm and held it high as he moved back to the wounded Griffin; he made a show of placing it on the seat. Then he reached to the back of the seat, pulled his sword out and smiled at the Mongol. The Mongol gave a little bow and started walking toward Ball; the battle below them had slowed and the gunfire had almost ceased.

Ball moved to the left, away from the Griffin and stood ready; the short sword in his right hand. The Mongol charged and swung his blade at Mad Jack's head. Ball parried with the flat of his double-edged sword sending the Mongol's blade at a different angle and ducked. The Mongol recovered and backed away; a smile returned to his lips.

Just a short distance away, Sanderson was locked in a grappling match with a Mongol about his same size. The Mongol's firearm was empty; he had discarded it and pulling his dagger had closed on Sanderson with a vengeance. Sanderson had blocked the initial swing with his rifle, the impact of the blade shattering the stock. Sanderson dropped the useless rifle and pulled his combat knife. The two now stood locked together; neither with an advantage and neither able to turn loose of the other for another attack. The Mongol was wiry, strength coming from desperation; his foul breath blowing into Sanderson's face with exertion.

Rourke saw the struggle and pulled his Detonics with his right hand. He was still firing the M-16 A12 on full auto at six Mongols closing on him when he snap fired a .45 slug into the chest of the man fighting Sanderson; the man staggered back dropping his dagger. Rubenstein dropped another Mongol with the Schmeisser and pushed his wire frame glasses back in place before splattering the head of a charging, sword-wielding Mongol. He spun violently to the right as a slug passed through his right leg, breaking the femur. "Go, go John, find Natalia."

Sanderson pulled back and then charged the man, driving his own blade into the man's stomach and jerking it upward. The point penetrated the man's heart, but he didn't die quickly; he struggled to attack Sanderson with his teeth. A few more heartbeats were required before the man slumped to the ground and Sanderson pulled the nine-inch blade out of his gut. Wiping it on the man's tunic, Sanderson turned to survey the battle.

Out of sight from the camp, a silent and deadly dance of steel continued between Mad Jack and his Mongol. Both blades flashed and the ring of steel on steel rang out. *The son of a bitch is good,* Mad Jack thought. Both men backed away from the fight, neither had scored first blood yet. Breathing deeply, they walked in a large circle facing each other, waiting. The Mongol whistled and his horse walked over to him. The Mongol pulled an animal skin bladder from the saddle. He stepped back and stuck his blade in the ground, uncorked the bladder, and took a drink; his eyes never leaving Mad Jack's.

Jack dropped the point of his sword and relaxed as he watched the Mongol. The Mongol finished his drink, corked the bladder's stopper, and held it forward in an offer to his opponent. Mad Jack smiled and nodded. The Mongol threw the bladder; Jack caught it with his left hand, pulled the cork and took a sip. The fermented goat wine stung his mouth but warmed his belly. Corking the bladder, he threw it back to the Mongol who nodded approval and tossed the bladder away.

Pulling his sword up, he looked at Jack. Jack smiled and gave a slight bow while raising his sword back into position. The Mongol charged, the wicked blade held high for a final stroke. The stroke came at Jack on his side; he sidestepped forty-five degrees to his right and deflected the attack with the forte, the third of the blade closest to the guard. He flicked his wrist letting his pummel go over his opponent's wrist, while stepping forty-five degrees to the left. Disengaging his blade, he pulled it back and thrust low into the Mongol's gut. For an instant the two men stood motionless, then the Mongol's knees buckled and he fell. It was over.

Chapter Sixteen

Rourke stuck the Detonics in his belt, changed rifle magazines and started forward to the nearest tent. Inside he saw the bodies—Natalia wasn't one of them. He pulled out and ran to the next tent; still no sign of her. Then behind and inside the third tent, he saw her. "Paul, over here," he screamed.

She lay covered in blood, partially hidden under one of the Mongols. Beside her lay another Mongol; his throat was ripped out. Rourke jerked the dead man off of her and pulled the Bali-Song from the man's chest. She had cut the man twice; the first cut had opened his stomach, dumping a huge volume of blood and his intestines on her and the ground. The second thrust was to his heart.

Kneeling, Rourke took a deep breath before feeling for a pulse in her neck—it was weak but it was there. "Medic," Rourke shouted. "Medic, get your ass in here!" A Navy Corpsman knelt next to Rourke, took one look and went to Natalia. Rourke stood up, getting out of the way. "Doc!" Rourke said harshly. The Corpsman worked silently, ignoring him. Rourke said a silent prayer and wondered, *How will I tell Michael and the kids?* He pulled one of his thin black cigars but didn't light it. While he wiped the blood and gore from the Bali-Song's blade and handle on the pants of the man she had killed, the Corpsman continued to work on Natalia.

Finally the Corpsman sat back on his heels and looking over his shoulder said, "She's lost a lot of blood. I've put an IV in to replace her blood volume; there may be damage to both her skull and cervical spine. We'll need x-rays to be sure. I've stabilized her neck with this collar. She's been beaten and she's dehydrated and needs surgery. But I think... I think Dr. Rourke, she's going to be okay. We need to get one of the ATPAAVs down here and get her back to Mid-Wake as soon as possible."

Rourke nodded, gave silent thanks to God and said, "You stay with her, as of right now I'm holding you personally responsible for her welfare." The Corpsman nodded and went back to work as Rourke stepped outside and waved for Rubenstein to send the all clear signal and bring his ATPAAV down to the camp. He held up a clenched fist with his thumb extended, the signal he and Paul had worked out if Natalia was alive. Then he pulled his battered Zippo and lit the cigar; he noticed his hand was shaking just a bit.

Rubenstein's leg wound had been bandaged and a field splint applied; he hobbled and was half carried by the other team medic to Rourke's side. "How is she?"

"Hurt but I think she'll survive. The medic thinks so and he pretty well confirmed my initial examination. We have to get her back."

"Any other members of the expedition make it?"

Rourke shook his head, "My focus was finding her, but I don't think so. Did you get the message out?"

Rubenstein nodded and walked painfully back to the right side of Rourke's Griffin, "I assume you're driving."

"Yeah," Rourke said pulling the fold-out stretcher from the back of the ATPAAV. "As soon as we can, load her." He glanced up the hill. Mad Jack Ball was walking toward Rourke, his sword still dripping blood. "Colonel, you look like hell," Rourke said.

"Take a look at the other guy," Ball smiled and raised his right hand; the severed head of the Mongol rider in it. "Got shot down by this fellow," he said explaining the fight to Rourke. When he finished, Ball spun the head by its long hair braid and heaved it off into the distance.

"Did you locate your daughter-in-law and is she alive?"

"Yes," Rourke said. "She's injured but we have her stabilized. It looks like the rest of her team was butchered. Sanderson is checking though."

Ball nodded, "I'm glad she's going to survive. How long before we move out?"

"Should be about…" Rourke glanced at his Rolex, "shouldn't be more than a few minutes."

"Then, I don't have very long to complete my mission." He pulled a small rectangular device from his breast pocket and flipped it down; a soft beeping sounded. "I better get started. Where was she found?"

Rourke pointed at the tent where he had found Natalia; Ball took off at a jog. Fifteen minutes later, Natalia bandaged and tied to the stretcher, was loaded onto the roof of the Griffin; an IV bag hung from one of the crash bars. Sanderson and his men checked the other tents, he looked at Rourke and just shook his head; Natalia's archeology team members were all dead. Rourke nodded and signaled it was time to go. It would be a long trip back to Mid-Wake but not as long as he had feared. Natalia was alive—at least for right now.

Ball bummed a ride back with Rourke; he stretched out in the cargo area behind the seats. "I found what I came for," he said padding his pocket.

"Colonel," Rourke started.

"John, would you just call me Jack?"

Rourke focused on the drive, "Absolutely Jack, about that short sword of yours. What is it?" Rourke asked pointing at the sword, "Am I correct, it is a modified version of the Roman Gladius?"

Ball smiled, "You are, but I worked several changes into this design, especially the hilt, grip and pummel. It is modeled on the Gladius Hispaniensis, or Spanish Gladius. The Romans placed a lot of emphasis with the sword. I wanted one that would cut and slash. All types of the Gladius were perfectly good at cutting if necessary, though this one was definitely best since it was longer, twenty-five to twenty-seven-inch blade. I split the difference and have a twenty-six-inch blade and a different style of hilt and pummel."

"I try to practice daily using a double-weight training model. While the classic attack involved knocking an opponent off-balance then a very fast thrust to the belly with the sword, I incorporate more of the medieval fencing and Japanese Wakizashi techniques."

Rourke nodded and thought for a moment, when he looked back at Mad Jack, he was sound asleep; his body bouncing with the movement of the Griffin. Rourke smiled to himself, *Yeah Mad Jack fits.*

Chapter Seventeen

The older gentleman stood outside a door in Baton Rouge, Louisiana, stroking his heavy mustache. Baton Rouge had climbed out of the apocalyptic destruction after the Night of the War and reestablished itself as a trade center between the wild areas that remained on both sides of the Mississippi and the few commercial areas that remained.

Confirming the address from a note card, he leaned heavily on the ebony cane with a sterling handle, opened the door and walked in. "Hello," he said to the secretary. "I don't have an appointment but if the owner is in, might I speak with him?"

She dialed an extension number and said into the handset, "A gentleman would like to speak with you, Sir. Okay, will do." Hanging up she gestured to the older man, "It is the door at the end of the hall, he said to come on in."

William Robert "Beaux Diddley" Delys, pronounced like the last part of the French emblem, the fleur-de-lys, rose from his desk and went to the door; he was casually dressed in slacks and a sports coat. "Hello Sir, I'm Beaux Delys. How can I help you?"

"Sir, I believe I have need of your services. But first I would like to interview you if you don't mind. My needs call for... shall I say, special considerations." He did not offer his name, but the handshake was firm and confident.

"Sit down and fire away," Delys said. He was used to being interviewed by potential clients. After all, trust and confidentiality were absolutely necessary in his line of work. "Would you care for coffee?"

The man sat down, "Yes, black please."

Delys punched the intercom, "Two cups Sally, black for both, please."

The old man scoured the citations and certifications on the wall as they waited. A gentle knock came at the door and the secretary entered with a tray carrying two coffees. She handed the first cup to the client, the second to her boss. "Thank you Sally," Delys said and she left.

"Mr. Delys," the older man said once Sally had closed the door to the office, "I hope you understand the need..." he said, pausing. "Shall I say the need for discretion of the highest order during our conversation?" Delys nodded and for the next hour, Delys fielded the usual questions he was so used to. Finally, the older man nodded with finality and said, "Then for our current purposes you may call me Otto Gruber. I'm confident that this nom de plume will be penetrated by you eventually, but by that time, I'm sure it will be irrelevant. I believe you were with the Honolulu Police Department originally, is that correct?"

Delys nodded, "Yes Sir, I suspect you knew that already. Additionally, by the nature of your questions, I can deduce you have already conducted a pretty thorough background check on me. That indicates you have a need for someone with discretion and some experience in covert operations. Am I correct?"

"You are," the older man said. Reaching in an inside coat pocket he pulled out a single index card. "I need to know if you can personally deliver this card to the gentleman whose name is on the reverse."

Delys reached across the desk taking the card, he sat back down before he read it. Glancing down at the card, Delys said under his breath, "Holy shit..." Looking up after almost a minute of staring at the card, Delys cleared his throat. "You realize this will require some... finesse?"

The older gentleman smiled, "I do Mr. Delys, I do. You may call me at this number when the card is delivered." Gruber slid another card across the desk. "You are to give this number to the recipient. I have already purchased a plane ticket for you." He slid a small envelope across the desk followed by a larger one. "There will be some travel expenses incurred; I believe this should cover your expenses and time. Additionally, I would like to place you on retainer. It is probable there will be additional requirements and for the duration of this arrangement I must insist your total attention and time must be at my disposal. Is that a problem?"

Delys stood again and reached over to accept the heavy manila envelope. A phone number was printed on the front; inside he counted six bundles of currency wrapped with a simple mustard colored paper band. By that marking strap, Delys knew each bundle would—or should—contain $10,000 in $100 bills. Delys shook his head, "No Sir, I don't believe that will be a problem. I assume you wish me to begin immediately?"

The older man nodded, "You may advise me of the details at the number on the larger envelope. He stood, extended his hand and said, "I will be waiting for his response, tell him that please." Standing, the older man said, "May I ask you one final question? I understand you go by the nickname of Beaux Diddley, why?"

Delys smiled, "One of my old partners stuck me with that; it's a play on my last name. The original Bo Diddley was a rhythm and blues singer, rock and roll pioneer, guitarist and songwriter in the early part of the twentieth century. In old American slang, bo diddly means 'absolutely nothing' and diddly is short for diddly-squat, or 'nothing' and bo meant 'a lot.' I changed the spelling to Beaux to compliment my French heritage and correspond to my last name. That's the whole story."

Otto Gruber, former president of the German Republic, smiled, shook Delys' hand and left the office, closing the door behind him. Delys picked up the card again and reread the message's two short sentences. "Jew, call me. The Nazi." There was a phone number at the bottom and on the reverse, a man's name was printed neatly, it read "Paul Rubenstein."

He glanced at the departure time on the ticket then at his watch. He would have to hurry. Pocketing the larger bundle, he opened his office closet and pulled out his "go bag," he kept for emergency travel. On the way out he told Sally, "Cancel the rest of my appointments. I need you to clear my schedule for the next ten days. I'll be leaving this afternoon and will check in from the road. Reassign any critical assignments among the team."

He made the flight with only minutes to spare.

Chapter Eighteen

Colonel Thorne couldn't sleep; a single thought kept running through his mind, *How do I turn the craft on? Maybe we're making this more complicated than it needs to be. Simple is always better.* He stopped tossing, got up and dressed. Walking from the Bachelor's Officers Quarters, he ran through the idea again and again. *I wonder, could it be that easy?*

The guard at the hanger saluted, "How you doing, Colonel? Your duty day is starting pretty early, isn't it Sir?"

"Couldn't sleep Sergeant, I want to try something," Thorne said returning the salute. At the Entry Control Point, Thorne handed over his Restricted Area Badge to the guard and received an exchange badge system to wear while his was in the hanger. Flight Surgeon Dr. Dalton was coming down the stairs as Thorne entered the office section of the hanger, "What are you doing here Colonel?"

"Doc, I have been thinking. Take me to the craft." Dalton took him to the hanger floor where the egg-shaped craft stood. "Give me a minute alone in there will you?" Thorne said. "I want to try something; probably won't work but I need to know."

Thorne walked through the hatch and sat down in the pilot's seat. He swiveled it around and sat there looking at the blank control panel. "Feels right," he said aloud as he settled into the seat, "Feels right." He reached out with his left hand and laid it on the surface of the panel, nothing happened. He moved his right hand and laid it on the surface, still nothing. He pulled them back and sat there for a moment thinking. Then he laid both hands at the same time on the panel and thought, *On.*

Instantly, a holographic image sprang into view. He jerked back in surprise and the image vanished. "Whoa, I didn't expect that," he said. Wiping his hands on his pants' leg he did it again and the image returned; this time he left his hands in place. He thought, *Systems*, and data began to stream across the hologram. *That's good*, he thought, *it is in English.* The order of the data was different from what he was used to but it was all there. Taking a deep breath, he thought, *Remain on standby.*

Standing up, he went to the hatch and hollered out, "Doc, have you got a camera?"

"In my office."

"Get it and come in here, hurry. Make sure the camera has good batteries and a new memory card." Dalton took off at a run returning in less than ten minutes with the camera, slightly out of breath.

"What now?" he asked.

Thorne sat back down and said, "Get the camera ready and watch this." Placing his hands again on the panel he thought, *Resume.* The holographic image sprang into being.

"Holy crap!" Dalton exclaimed. "How did you do that?"

"See if it registers on the camera," was all Thorne said.

"Yeah, it does."

"Then start taking pictures, damn it. Don't use the flash." For the next thirty minutes, the camera snapped again and again. Finally Thorne thought, *Off,* the image faded and he swiveled the pilot seat around. Sweat glistened across his forehead as he said, "Whew, it worked."

Dalton shook his head, "I don't know how you did it but you sure made something happen."

Thorne stood up and followed Dalton out of the craft, "Let's get to your office, I want to see those photographs."

"How did you figure it out?" Dalton asked as they headed off.

"I kept thinking about what you said the other day, that it was as though the pilot had to 'wear' the craft to fly it. I couldn't shake the idea. I couldn't see how each of these craft would be designed for individual pilots. It had to be simpler than that. Flying is flying... we were over thinking the way to do it; I just simplified the thinking process."

The next day, Thorne and Dalton briefed the Chief of Staff, General Sullivan, on their progress. Sullivan said, "I have to get back to headquarters. I will expect a briefing on your progress tomorrow."

Chapter Nineteen

The Griffins landed close to the VTOL transport planes and were loaded. The wounded, including Natalia, were loaded on one bird with Rourke and Rubenstein. The flight back to rendezvous with surface ships from Mid-Wake took almost six hours.

The plane carrying Natalia and the other wounded landed on the first of two carriers, followed shortly thereafter by the Combat Air Control planes; the other transport landed on the second. The wounded were off-loaded and transported to the medical facilities below deck. The two ships and their escorts then steamed away at flank speed for the underwater city of Mid-Wake's coordinates.

President of the United States, Michael Rourke, had been the first to meet the VTOL and helped off-load his wife and followed her below deck. John Rourke followed as Natalia was rushed directly into the operating room. An hour later, John said, "Michael, I'm going to check on Paul and the others. Then I'm going to get a smoke, I can't stand this waiting." Michael just nodded and said, "I understand, I'll let you know as soon as I know. Dad, thanks for everything you did."

Rourke nodded and walked down the passage way. He had passed a hatch when he heard, "John, how's Natalia?" Turning back he looked in and saw Paul lying in a bed; his right leg already in a cast and hung up by a cable system.

"Don't know yet Paul," Rourke said. "She's still in surgery. What did they say about your leg?"

"It'll heal but it's going to take a while. The slug cracked the femur on its way through, pretty well messed the muscles but they've put that back together. Doctor suspects I may have some nerve damage but we'll have to let it heal before we'll know for sure. How's Michael doing?"

"Seems to be holding it together, that's all any of us can do until the doctors tell us more. You get some rest, I still have to call Emma and let her tell the kids. I'll check on you later."

Paul nodded, "Ask her to tell Annie I'm okay and I'll call her or see her soon. Any idea when we'll get to Mid-Wake?"

Rourke glanced at his Rolex Submariner, "Should just be another two hours or so, I think. I'll double check with the Captain and let you know. Now rest." Rourke walked out and headed to the starboard observation platform. He stepped out, the sea air pleasantly shocking his senses. He pulled the last of his cigars and turning, cupped the battered Zippo and puffed.

"You have another one of those?" a voice said.

Rourke turned and saw Sanderson coming out of the hatch. "Nope, last one but you're welcome to share it." Rourke took another puff and passed it over to Sanderson who inhaled deeply, letting the smoke out in a long exhale.

"How are your men doing?" John asked.

Sanderson took another puff and passed the cigar back, "All of the wounded have been checked; most will be okay but Franklin—the one who took a slug in his back—is still guarded. How's the lady doing?"

"No word yet, she's still in surgery."

Sanderson nodded and the two were silent as they smoked the rest of the cigar. Both lost in their own thoughts. The ship's speaker squawked and a voice said, "Dr. Rourke please report to sick bay." Rourke took a last drag and handed the cigar to Sanderson, "I'll see you later, finish this."

Sanderson nodded and said, "Good luck, hope it all works out." Rourke went below; Sanderson smoked the rest of the cigar before flipping it overboard and high in the air. He watched it until the wind grabbed it, jerking it toward the rear of the ship; he never saw it splash into the ocean waves.

Chapter Twenty

Michael sat next to the bed watching her breath slowly, very slowly. Each time she exhaled it seemed an inordinate amount of time passed before she inhaled. Her face had been cleaned but was swollen, the left side particularly. Abrasions and bruises covered the rest of her face. A large bandage was wrapped around her forehead and another covered her damaged neck. With the bandages, bruising, and swelling, plus the tape holding an air line that ran down her nasal passage, he realized that if he had not known it was her... he wouldn't have recognized his own wife. Throughout the night the only sounds in the room were the sounds of the nurses checking her vitals, repeated visits from his father who also checked the charts, her vitals, the connections of IVs, and electrodes. When no one else was in the room, the only sound was the rhythmic beep... beep... beep of the heart monitor.

Chapter Twenty-One

"She is out of surgery," Rourke told Emma over the satellite phone. "We should be in Mid-Wake shortly. They'll transfer her to the main hospital; the next twelve to eighteen hours are the most critical."

"I called Sarah and told her what we knew," Emma said. "She's leaving within the hour for Honolulu; she wants to help keep the kids stable while we're waiting on word."

"That's fine," Rourke said. "It will help them I'm sure. How are you doing?" There was a long pause and he heard her take a deep breath.

"John, I'm scared. What if Natalia doesn't make it? What if she doesn't recover fully? How are the kids and Michael going to take that?"

"I know," he said, rubbing his eyes with one hand. "Honey, it is going to be what it is going to be. We'll all have to deal with it but we need to find out what the IT is. I don't know what else to say."

*****

Michael had dozed off. He had hardly slept since the report of the attack had reached his office nearly fifty-two hours earlier. He stirred—she had squeezed his hand. Looking over he saw her eyes were open, "Hello Baby, the Docs say you're going to be fine. You just need some rest." He wasn't positive but he thought she nodded slightly before drifting back to sleep. He studied her face and it seemed less drawn and her color, what he could see of it under the bandages and bruises, seemed better.

An hour and a half later, the ship was moored. Natalia, Rubenstein, and the more seriously injured were sent by ambulances and admitted to the Honolulu Medical Center. Those who were ambulatory were bused to Honolulu General. Along the way, Natalia went into cardiac arrest. It had taken the EMTs three tries with the defibrillator to get her back.

Chapter Twenty-Two

Paul Rubenstein borrowed Rourke's A.G. Russell Sting 1A and began cutting the lines holding his leg in the air while John kept the leg from falling. "Paul," John said, "you know this is against your doctor's orders."

"Yeah, I know." When he had cut the last line, John gently lowered the leg to the bed and Paul moved into a sitting position. Swinging his body to the right, Paul pulled himself erect and supported his weight on a walker. He was careful not to put any weight on his injured leg. Rourke had helped him out of bed, against the orders of the medical staff. Rourke moved the wheelchair behind Paul and braced it. Paul tried to ease himself down but ended up with a grimace of pain on his face, doing a butt flop into the chair.

"Damnit," Paul said through clenched teeth, then looked up at Rourke and nodded, "Let's go see her." Rourke pulled the chair back and eased it into the hallway; the steely eyes of the Director of Nursing locked him in her gaze. Rourke stared back and said quietly, "I know... I know. He made me do it, do you want to try and stop this guy?" The D.O.N. frowned and with a snort went back to her paperwork.

They went down the hallway to the right and stopped at the elevator. When it opened, Rourke pushed the chair inside and they rode the elevator up two floors. Rourke pushed Paul out of the elevator and stopped to hold the elevator door for another patient. When he turned back, Paul was gone, pushing himself down the ICU hallway and up to the nurse's station.

"Natalia Rourke. What room is she in?" Paul asked.

"Mrs. Rourke cannot have visitors, only family," the charge nurse said.

"Damnit," Paul shouted. "I am family, what room?" Rourke grabbed the handles of the wheelchair and started it moving. "I know where she's at Paul, calm down." Rubenstein didn't respond. When they rounded the next corner Paul knew what room she was in by the number of Secret Service agents around the door of room 342; he started propelling the chair himself. Rourke let him go. The agents looked at Rubenstein then looked at Rourke who nodded and flashed the okay sign to them and they stepped back; one agent opened the door for Paul.

Paul nodded his thanks and, taking a deep breath, rolled into the room. Michael looked up and said, "How are you Paul?"

"I'm fine," Rubenstein said. "How about her?"

"She woke up for a moment..." Michael checked his watch. "About twenty minutes ago for just a second then went back to sleep. We have to wait and see. She'll survive but those bastards hurt her Paul. They hurt her badly."

"I talked to your mom a little while ago when John called her," Paul said. "She's enroute to Honolulu to help with the kids. She sends her love to both of you. When do you expect the next report from the doctors?"

"I don't know," Michael said checking his watch. "Could be anytime but I'd say another hour at least."

"Alright, your dad's outside. I'm going to check in with Annie again. I spoke to her yesterday but I wanted to wait until I saw you and Natalia before I called back."

"Tell my kids I'll call them after the doctor gives us an update," Michael said. Paul nodded and wheeled about, he kicked the door and it opened, held in place by the same agent who had opened it for him.

Chapter Twenty-Three

Thorne took a deep breath before knocking on the office door. The door opened and General Sullivan smiled, "Come in Colonel."

"How are you Sir?" He noticed the Chief of Staff looked harried; stubble showed along his chin line and his face was drawn. He was in the same uniform he had worn the day before.

"Frankly Colonel, I'm concerned. Sit down please; we have to have a talk." Sullivan didn't return to his desk but walked to a file cabinet and removed a bottle of whiskey and two glasses, "Drink?"

"If you're offering... I'd be honored," Thorne said. *This must be serious,* he thought.

Sullivan nodded and poured two shots handing one to Thorne before he pulled a chair up and sat across from him. "I've looked at your record, Colonel. Command experience, combat experience, test pilot... You've made a career putting your ass on the line for this country."

Thorne shifted uncomfortably, "As you have, Sir."

Sullivan nodded, "So we have, Colonel... so we have. Cheers."

"Cheers, Sir." Thorne clicked glasses and sipped the warm whiskey.

Sullivan slugged down his drink and smiled. "Need you to do something, Rodney." The shift to his first name did not go unnoticed by Thorne.

"Sir?"

Sullivan flipped open a humidor on the coffee table and removed two cigars, clipped the tips and handed one to Thorne. "You realize this is not a social call Colonel."

Thorne took the cigar; he hadn't smoked in years. "Didn't figure it was, General."

Sullivan nodded, lit a match and offered it to Thorne. Thorne puffed, got the cigar going and nodded. Sullivan touched the match to his own cigar and puffed. "Here's where we're at. There is every probability we are about to be engaged on two fronts. One is conventional, the other isn't." Thorne sat quietly. "I need a straight, no BS answer. Can you fly the UFO?"

"Yes Sir, now that I figured out how to turn the damn thing on. I believe I can fly it."

Sullivan nodded, "How familiar are you with the old astronaut training?"

"Truthfully, it was not that different in many ways from our current flight training. With the exception of course of long term zero-gravity activities."

Sullivan smiled, "Correct. The effects of launching and landing had various effects on astronauts, with the most significant effects that occur being space motion sickness, orthostatic intolerance, and cardiovascular events. Stuff like that. Space motion sickness could occur within minutes of being in changing gravity environments. The symptoms ranged from drowsiness and headaches, to nausea and vomiting."

"About two-thirds of astronauts experienced space motion sickness, with effects rarely exceeding two days. There is a risk for post-flight motion sickness; however, this was only significant following long-duration space missions. During training, astronauts are familiarized with the engineering systems of the spacecraft. Not the least of which was orbital mechanics."

Thorne paused for a moment, "If my memory serves, virtual reality was used as a tool to immerse astronauts in many of the operational aspects."

The Chief of Staff nodded. "In the old days, the training took years. We don't have years. Let me tell you what we're thinking. This conversation is ultra secret, Colonel. Agreed?"

Thorne nodded and sat up straight, "Roger that Sir." Sullivan spoke uninterrupted for the next forty-five minutes.

Chapter Twenty-Four

A stern-faced physician stood at the end of Natalia's bed, deep in thought. "How's she doing doctor?" Paul asked.

Glancing up at the intrusion the doctor frowned, "What the hell are you doing here?" He turned to Rourke, "Is this your doing?"

John shook his head, "Couldn't stop him Doc. Answer the question, how is she doing?"

"Dr. Rourke, as you know from your own experience, medical science has advanced significantly from what you learned in your training. In the 'old days,' if you will allow that term, doctors were more like mechanics. We really had little understanding as to how the body worked and how disease states functioned. The old pharmaceutical companies created drugs to attack diseases. Those drugs took over and initiated repairs to the body. The reality we did not know then, is the body itself is its own best physician. It can literally defend itself against and repair damage that is done to the body, with the right fuel."

"The most important discovery for your immune system is something called glyconutrients. 'Glyco' means 'sweet' in Latin; these nutrients are long-chain complex carbohydrates or saccharides. Six of the eight essential glyconutrients are known to be missing in the modern diet due to over-farming, green-harvesting, food processing, and soil depletion caused by the Night of the War. What we now know is that these eight sugars, or glyconutrients, are necessary to build 'glycoprotein.'"

"Those are the hair-like structures on the outsides of our cells which enable cell-to-cell communication, right?" Rourke asked.

"Exactly, without adequate amounts of these eight sugars, the human body cannot function properly, as research has shown. Science and medicine have long tried to understand the code by which the cells in the body communicate with one another in order for its complex functions to occur. For example, how does your digestive system know which food components to absorb into the blood stream and which to ignore? Or which cells to attack and destroy and which to protect and nurture? That code has now been broken. This role is undertaken by glyconutrients. Researchers proclaim it to be the most important discovery in the history of medicine. The key to a long, healthy life."

"Following the Night of the War, Mid-Wake scientists were faced with feeding its population. One of the best sources of food nutrition was Chlorella. It is a single-cell fresh water green microalgae that is loaded with nutrients. It contains more nucleic acids, RNA and DNA, than any other food, which gives it a lot of energy producing potential. It is a great supplement to boost any diet lacking in green vegetables. Chlorella contains more chlorophyll than most plants, along with an impressive array of vitamins and minerals."

"It is also one of the most vibrant and energetic organisms on Earth, able to reproduce rapidly due to its highly active cellular components. These nutritious factors are called Chlorella Growth Factor, what we call CGF. CGF is a mix of its nucleic acids along with important glyconutrients or essential sugars. These are glucose, mannose, rhamnose, arabinose, galactose, and xylose as well as vital amino acids."

Rourke was drifting in thought, *Could it be that this is the missing part of the equation? Is this the science the aliens were using and the reason for the war with the Atlanteans?*

"Simply put," the Doctor continued, "Glyconutrition allows the cell-to-cell communication for the body to rapidly 'heal' itself. As you know, Mr. Rubenstein's broken femur would normally require immobilization and support and it would take six to eight weeks for the bone to knit itself back together. However, on this régime, he'll be mobile in six to eight days."

"What about Natalia?" Rubenstein asked again.

"From the physical damage she sustained, about the same amount of time will be necessary for her. Now, that will be the amount of time necessary to launch an aggressive physical rehabilitation. I cannot speak to her psychological damage."

Rourke shook his head, "That's amazing Doctor."

"What is amazing is it took so long for science and medicine to come together and figure how the body works and what a fantastic mechanism it really is. Glyconutrients are the key to effective cellular communication and proper cell function. They are not vitamins, minerals, amino acids, or enzymes, but are in a class of their own as nutritional supplementation. Simply, healthy cells lead to healthy tissue—healthy tissue leads to healthy organs—and healthy organs lead to healthy bodies."

Chapter Twenty-Five

Delys had checked into his hotel before trying to call Paul Rubenstein's phone. After identifying himself, he was told by a male voice, "There has been a slight accident. Mr. Rubenstein is not available at the moment. Can you call back tomorrow?" Delys said he would and left his contact information in the event Paul wanted to reach him. Delys wondered what had happened and how it would affect his own mission. After ordering room service, he climbed into the shower. As he was drying off someone knocked on his door, "Just a minute," he shouted as he slipped on a robe and walked barefoot to the door.

Expecting the room service attendant, he was surprised to see three men in dark suits with ear buds obvious, standing there. "Mr. Delys, may we come in?" the nearest one said flashing his Secret Service credentials. Delys almost didn't recognize him, then with a grin opened the door and said, "Tim Shaw, you old reprobate what are you doing here? And when did you sign on with the Secret Service?"

Shaw entered and the other two waited outside, he wasn't smiling. Delys was puzzled, "Am I in trouble?"

Shaw took off his fedora and threw it on the bed, "I don't know Beaux but I need to ask you some questions. What are you doing here for a starter? And why did you try to contact Paul Rubenstein?"

"I'm on a job, Tim," Delys said and he resumed drying his hair. "A client of mine wants me to deliver a message to Mr. Rubenstein. That's the long and short of it."

"Paul has been in a little 'accident.'" Shaw said. "He's not available."

"That's what I was told when I called," Delys said.

"Who's your client and what is the message?"

Delys shook his head, "Tim, you know that information is confidential. I don't have to give it to you."

Shaw nodded and looked for an ash tray as he dug a cigarette out of the pack. Finding none, he picked up a coffee cup from next to the maker and went to the sink where he put a half inch of water in it. "Okay, Beaux," Shaw said after he had lit the cigarette. "I'm not going to dance around with you. Here it is, the only way you're going to see Paul Rubenstein is through me. The only way that is going to happen is for you to tell me what it is about... everything. Or, you can get back on the plane tomorrow and tell your client how you failed in your mission. Got it?"

Delys suddenly realized he had stumbled into something more complicated than just delivering a message—and he didn't know what it was. "Give me a minute to get my clothes on, Tim," Delys said and walked into the bathroom. Shortly after, he came out in slacks and a t-shirt but still barefooted. Sliding on his moccasins, Delys went to his briefcase, opened it and pulled the card out. "Here's the message, Tim. I never met the guy before, never saw him before. Don't know who he is, but he said Rubenstein would know him. Got paid cash up-front and unless he contacts me, I don't expect to see or hear from him again."

"Describe him to me," Shaw said as he read the simple message of the note, "Jew, call me. The Nazi." Turning the card over he saw the phone number scrawled neatly in long hand.

Delys cleared his throat, "Older white guy, thin and tall; slightly over six feet. Has a heavy mustache, grey hair... I believe a wig." Delys thought for a moment before adding, "He has a pulsating vein right here." Delys pointed at his own temple. "I'd say early sixties now, but in his day I'd say he was a real badass; probably still a handful. I do have a picture from our office surveillance video if that will help." Delys pulled the photo from the briefcase and handed it to Shaw. "That's all I've got, honest Tim."

Shaw studied it and said, "I assume your client didn't know he was getting his picture taken..."

Delys smiled. "They never do."

Shaw nodded, "Okay, IF you get to see Rubenstein it won't be today—day after tomorrow at the earliest. I'll convey the message for you and if he wants to talk to you, I'll take you there but no promises, agreed?"

"Look Tim," Delys said. "Honestly, I'm not emotionally invested in this. If you tell me the message has been delivered, I'll head home tomorrow. My job will be finished."

"No Beaux, Paul may very well want to talk to you. Stand by here, I'll be calling you." A knock came at the door and Delys opened it; finally, room service had arrived. Tim picked up his hat, "Good to see you, Beaux."

Delys stuck out his hand as Tim Shaw exited the room, turning to return the handshake. "Good to see you again, Tim."

The room service attendant looked a little puzzled, "Is everything alright, Sir?"

"I sure hope so, just set everything on the coffee table, please."

*****

Shaw waited until he and his men were out of the hotel before activating the sleeve microphone and speaking into his hand. "When are they coming back here?" He listened then said, "No, the one I'm concerned about is Rubenstein." He got his answer, "Roger, we're headed back to the office."

Chapter Twenty-Six

Following his instructions, the room service attendant set up Beaux's supper on the coffee table. The T-bone steak was grilled to perfection; a small loaf of artisan bread, a baked potato—heavy on the butter—a side salad and apple pie a' la mode completed the meal. Delys poured a generous glass of red wine, sat on the couch and punched the television remote. "Alright," he said out loud, "just what the doctor ordered." A private detective marathon was running with old reruns of Peter Gunn, Magnum P.I. and his favorite, Mannix.

Delys always pictured himself rather like Mannix or Joseph R. "Joe" Mannix if you wanted to be correct. A regular guy, without pretense, but a storehouse of proverbs to fall back on in conversation; Mannix was noted for taking a lot of physical punishment. Before the series ended he had been shot and wounded over a dozen separate times, and knocked unconscious around fifty-five times. Delys had made the choice to try and avoid that part.

Delys thought his story read like a bad novel. Following his retirement from law enforcement and a bloody divorce, Delys returned to his home state, Louisiana. He had gotten into this business rather by accident; truth be known—he had been bored. Ken LaBorde, an old high school friend had stopped over for a few beers and noticed Delys seemed distracted. "Waz da matter wid chu?" Even after all of this time, the Cajun dialect had not died off in Louisiana.

Delys said, "Man, I gotta have a game."

"What you mean?" LaBorde asked.

"I am going out of my mind. Don't get me wrong, retirement is good but I'm caught up on all my honey-dos and I am just stinking bored. The money is not important, sure it would be nice to make some but I'm not looking for another career. I just want something to keep my mind functioning, I need a game."

That evening he was channel surfing and came across a rerun, of all things, an old private eye show called Peter Gunn. The next day he started digging; he had worked with PIs while at Honolulu PD, though he really never cared for them. *Might be a fun gig,* he thought. To qualify for a license a person had to be of legal age, be a citizen of the United States or a resident alien with proper documentation to work in the United States. There couldn't be any felony convictions or crimes involving moral turpitude. He hadn't been declared incompetent by reason of mental defect or disease. *Hmmm, I think I could do this.*

Later he had told LaBorde, "I knew I was good on the qualifications..."

LaBorde smiled. "I don't know about that turpitude or mental defect..."

Delys smiled. "The big question was funding for the licenses and cost to set up an agency. The answer to that literally fell into my hands. I had picked up an old desk at a garage sale. Cleaning it out I found several old coins wedged in the corners of two of the drawers. I contacted a coin dealer I knew; when I showed him the coins, the guy almost had a heart attack."

"All of the coins had some silver content but not anything special. Two however, a pair of dimes, were 1916 Mercury dimes with a mint mark of 'D' for Denver. The dealer explained there had only been 264,000 minted in a seriously limited run. 'They were the most valuable mercury dimes ever minted! The numismatic value far exceeded its intrinsic or monetary value. One in poor condition will be valued at somewhere around $1,000, while one in perfect condition can bring $30,000 plus.'"

"I had two in that condition. Four hours later, I had just under $65,000 laid in my hands and the dealer had two mercury dimes in his. The term, paradigm, describes distinct concepts or thought patterns in scientific concepts but it was a pair of dimes that had financed my dream, so it became The Paradimes Detective Agency and as they say, 'The rest is history...'"

Before the actor played Mannix, he had starred for one season on another detective show, Tight Rope. He played Nick Stone, a police undercover agent who infiltrated organized crime to expose the leaders and their plots. His name changed with each episode in order to protect him. The character carried a Walther PP in a shoulder rig and a backup .38 revolver in a "small of the back" holster. When the bad guys searched him on the show and found the Walther they never went any further in the search. Delys never cared for the .32 caliber and instead opted for the new Lancer PPK/S in 9mm and their Model 60 reproduction of the Smith and Wesson Police Chief.

*****

The phone on the desk jingled and Delys walked over and answered, "Beaux Delys."

"You finished with your meal?" It was Tim Shaw's voice.

"Just about, what do you need?"

"I need a drink; you want to meet me in the bar downstairs?" Shaw asked.

"Sure. When?"

"I'll be there in about an hour," Shaw said and broke the connection.

Chapter Twenty-Seven

Natalia was still under heavy pain medication. The head of the National Security Agency, Harmon Knowles, sat with John Rourke inside a secure conference room at the Capital Building. Rourke said, "Okay Mr. Knowles, I've laid out my questions and would like some straight answers."

Knowles cleared his throat, "Here is the reality, Mr. Rourke. Yes, several governments including our own knew for a long time of the existence of the Aliens. Long before the Night of the War those governments made the decision not to tell the populace the truth out of fear of their reaction. Fear of mass panic, like that which occurred when Orson Wells broadcast the War of the Worlds as a Halloween special over the Columbia Broadcasting System's radio network back in 1938."

"That broadcast, which ran slightly over an hour, was presented as a series of simulated news bulletins which had many convinced an actual alien invasion by Martians was in fact going on. The hysteria was enhanced because the show ran without commercial breaks. This added to the program's realism. Following this broadcast there was widespread outrage in the media and panic by certain listeners, who had believed the events described in the program were real."

Knowles took a sip of coffee, gaining the time to continue his thoughts. "Even with the twenty-eight changes required by CBS's censors, the script was 'too realistic.' Most involved changing the names of real places, institutions and officials to something fictional—the result proved that horrifying reaction and fears of the public. This set the course of non-information and even misinformation that continued for almost sixty years. In actuality, that radio broadcast was a test, devised by our government to... I guess you would call it, to test the reaction of the general public."

"The test was successful, it proved true the speculation that the general public would react with... shall we say predictably negative responses. The whole concept of 'coming clean' and announcing contact with an alien race was scrapped and from that time forward kept from the public. When war finally came, most records—even entire facilities—disappeared and were replaced with half-truths, down-right lies, and conspiracy theories. That is where it was kept—until now and frankly, the veil of secrecy has been obliterated."

"Yeah," Rourke said, "and now we have to deal with the reality; and how exactly how do you guys propose doing that?"

Chapter Twenty-Eight

Delys was seated at a table in the hotel bar when Tim Shaw walked in. Shaw spotted him and walked toward the table as Delys stood. Delys extended his hand, "Tim, you look like crap. What are you drinking?"

They shook hands; Shaw pulled off his trench coat and laid it and his fedora on the third chair. "Scotch, neat."

Delys waved for the waiter. "Would you bring a double Scotch, neat and a refill of my drink? And go ahead and send over the appetizers, please." Turning back to Shaw he asked, "Been one of those days?"

Shaw nodded, "You have no idea. You know I always thought I just need two tools to make it through life: WD-40 and duct tape. If something doesn't move and should, use the WD-40. If it shouldn't move but does, use the duct tape. Man, life used to be simple."

"Yeah," Delys said as the waiter brought the drinks. "I've always figured if you can't fix it with a hammer, you've got an electrical problem."

Shaw picked up his drink, "Sorry about that stuff before, Beaux. Things are pretty intense right now."

"I figured you would tell me what the deal was when you were ready. It's not a problem," Delys said bumping glasses with Shaw. "It is good to see you again, Tim. I'm not prying, but I'll listen if you want to share. Maybe I can help?"

Shaw swallowed, the Scotch instantly warming his gut, "Before we start... Beaux my circumstances are a lot different right now." He pulled a sheet of paper from his inside coat pocket. "This is a non-disclosure agreement; I have to ask you to sign it before we can talk."

Delys looked seriously at Shaw and took the paper. "Tim, you know anything you say to me stays between you and me, right?"

"Yeah, I do, Beaux I don't have any choice. This is big."

Delys nodded and signed without reading the NDA. "Okay, fire away."

Shaw put the NDA back in his pocket. "Thanks, here's the deal. I spoke with Paul Rubenstein by satellite phone and gave him the message. Seems that this old acquaintance from his and John's earlier exploits is none other than the former president of the German Republic—Otto Croenberg."

"I thought Croenberg was killed a couple of weeks ago in a car wreck outside of New Munich City?" Delys said.

Shaw nodded, set down his empty glass and signaled the waiter for another round. "That appears to be what Croenberg wants the rest of the world to believe. But Paul confirmed the message."

"Where is Mr. Rubenstein, when do I meet him?"

"Paul is in the hospital," Shaw said. "Right now, I can't tell you any more than that. I will let him know what is going on and if he wants to see you..." Shaw let the sentence trail off. The waiter arrived with the drinks and appetizers. Shaw continued, "Beaux it looks like you have been pulled into something of a mystery."

Delys frowned, "Do you have any idea what is going on?"

Shaw answered the question with another question, "What do you know about an EMP?"

"You're talking about an electro-magnetic pulse attack?"

Shaw nodded.

"I know it was feared they would destroy America's defenses before the Night of the War, leaving the U.S. in a technology world equivalent to the 1800s. An EMP weapon is supposed to be able to take out electronic devices including targeting, communications, navigation, and sensor systems. All of that would cripple our ability to defend ourselves against a land invasion. The more we use electronic devices, the more dependent we are on them, and the more vulnerable we are to this sort of threat."

Shaw smiled, "What would you say if I told you a company had developed a device that can withstand the EMP... AND identify an attacker in the aftermath."

"How?" Delys asked. "You can't smell, taste, or feel EMP radiation. As I understand it, EMPs can be unleashed by nuclear explosions as well as by solar storms and devices. The low level electromagnetic pulse can jam electronics systems temporarily or mega bursts that would utterly fry electric and electronic equipment; any sort of pulse would be bad news."

"Planes would fall from the skies, transportation could come to a screeching halt, water and sewage systems could suddenly cease to work, and on and on. An EMP can destroy electrical components permanently and they can't be repaired." He paused for effect.

"Yes, this team has developed technology to detect the source of an EMP attack, including an attack's strength, frequency, and direction. It uses four specialized antennae mounted on a tripod, each of which covers a ninety degree quadrant. In a monitoring station, a computer takes the data, analyzes it and then provides answers on screen—where the blast came from and how long it lasted. EMP blasts are a real threat. A nuclear detonation high in the atmosphere above the U.S. can create a pulse across all of North America. These weapons are attractive not just to foreign militaries, but to terrorist and criminal organizations as well. Several groups are apparently using Russian technology to develop electromagnetic pulse weapons capable of paralyzing military electronic equipment."

"It is said the high-power microwave weapons are small enough to fit in a suitcase and they can disable smaller targets like neighborhoods, banks, and stock exchanges. These devices can be used to cause confusion or to infiltrate secure areas by disabling alarm systems. An attacker would merely need to get within a few yards of a target and push a button to unleash the pulse."

"Recently in Germany, thieves used electromagnetic waves to defeat a limousine security system. We have had several incidents here in the last days."

Shaw's cell phone rang, he stood and excused himself. A few minutes later, he returned and told Delys, "Paul is calling Croenberg's number this evening. Maybe tomorrow he can let us know what is happening."

"I take that to mean we'll talk to him then?" Beaux said.

"Maybe, that's up to him; Croenberg for sure though."

"That's fine; all I was supposed to do was facilitate contact between them." Delys leaned back and said, "Okay, shifting gears. How did you get this gig anyway?"

Shaw stuffed a potato skin in his mouth and took a swig of Scotch and told Delys the story. Finally, he wrapped it up and said, "I saw a quote by John Steinbeck, it went something like this, '... peace, not war, is the destroyer of men; tranquility rather than danger is the mother of cowardice, and not need but plenty brings apprehension and unease... the longed-for peace, so bitterly achieved, created more bitterness than ever did the anguish of achieving it.' I can tell you this; it has been a hell of ride so far. How's your agency doing?"

Delys smiled, it was like old times again and they had moved to shop talk. "It's been busy but lucrative. Simple divorce cases mostly. You know the kind that don't turn out so simple. I just wrapped one up on a National Guard Lieutenant Colonel who hooked up with a female Staff Sergeant, much to the chagrin of his wife. In spite of her efforts, the bosses at the National Guard at the time chose, for whatever reasons, to not prosecute her husband on any charges. He eventually made full Colonel and retired to South Georgia."

"What about the dame?" Shaw asked.

Delys smiled, "Final justice, she skated on my case, but she kept cycling through higher ranking men and kept moving up in rank. Another angry wife caught her with her husband and shot her in the crotch with a .38."

Shaw said, "Ah, yes. Ain't justice a bitch. You know some people are like Slinkies, not really good for anything but they bring a smile to your face when they're pushed down the stairs."

"Amen," Delys laughed and stood. "I'll be in the room if you need me or at this number." He handed a card to Shaw, they shook hands and said goodbye.

Chapter Twenty-Nine

Delys entered the elevator in the lobby, holding the door for a small man running to catch it.

"Thanks," the little man said as he stepped in.

Delys nodded, pushed the button for his floor and asked, "Which floor?"

"Twenty-five," the small man said as he stepped to the back of the elevator and leaned against the wall as it started moving. "Mr. Delys, please keep your hands where I can see them," a soft voice said in his ear as the hard muzzle of a gun was pressed to his spine. "I require some privacy for our discussion," the man said. Delys complied, took a deep breath pushed the fog of his drinks with Shaw away and gathered his faculties. The little man patted Delys down, pulling the PPK/S from Beaux's shoulder rig. "Mr. Delys, I apologize for the method of our introduction, but I need to speak with you privately."

"Ever heard of scheduling an appointment on the phone?" Delys said over his shoulder, neither expecting nor receiving an answer. The elevator stopped on the twenty-fifth floor, a man stepped inside and the elevator began its descent to the parking garage.

"All is well?" he asked, receiving only a nod from the small man. The speaker looked at Delys and said, "Please relax Mr. Delys. We simply want to speak with you." Delys said nothing.

Exiting the elevator, Beaux was nudged forward. The man who had joined them dropped back a few feet and followed several paces behind. Another man, standing about twenty feet inside, nodded and led the small procession. They walked to a large, heavy black SUV with smoked windows. The large side door opened and Delys was pushed into a seat. The little man took a seat next to Beaux as his companion entered the passenger door. The third man slid the side door closed, walked around the SUV and climbed in the driver's seat and started the motor. The little man, still holding the silenced automatic in his right hand, pulled a small Meerschaum pipe, already packed with tobacco, and a lighter from his inside jacket pocket. Keeping his eye on Delys, he puffed until the Meerschaum was going to his content and then smiled. "My name is Aharon,

Aharon Friedman and I work for an organization that you would refer to as Nazi hunters."

"Well, Aharon. I'm just a private investigator and I'm sorry but I don't know any Nazis."

Friedman's eyes and voice went hard, "Ah, Mr. Delys, I am afraid that is either inaccurate or untrue. It is my job to determine which and I am very good at my job by the way. I understand you are here attempting to contact Paul Rubenstein."

"That is correct," Delys said. "I have a client who wants me to convey a message to Mr. Rubenstein."

"May I inquire what the message is?"

"He wants Rubenstein to call him. That is all I know."

Friedman nodded and puffed the pipe; the automatic in his right hand never wavered. "And you have no idea why your client wishes to speak to Mr. Rubenstein?"

"It's none of my business, Aharon. May I ask why it is any of yours?"

Friedman smiled, "Because Mr. Rubenstein, as you know, is Jewish and your client is none other than Otto Croenberg. Herr Croenberg, the former Neo-Nazi head of New Germany, recently faked his death. Mr. Rubenstein is quite likely the most famous member of the Jewish race and a compatriot of the Rourke family. My organization wishes to know if there is a threat to Rubenstein or the Rourkes. If so, my job is to eliminate that threat and determine if you are a part of that threat." Friedman left the statement open.

Chapter Thirty

The .38 snub in a "small of the back" holster had been missed by Friedman's search and it gave Beaux a degree of security as he explained how the man known as Otto Gruber had contacted him. "I now know that Gruber is Croenberg, but I didn't know that until just a few moments ago. That is all of the information I have Mr. Friedman." Beaux had managed to shift his position slightly by leaning his left elbow on the arm rest and laying his other hand next to his hip.

Friedman sat looking deep into Delys eyes before nodding. Finally laying the pistol on the seat next to him, he puffed the Meerschaum several times before saying, "I fear we may have a problem Mr. Delys." He dropped the magazine from Beaux's PPK/S before handing it back to him and nodded, "Trust me Mr. Delys, I am not your enemy but I fear the enemy is at the gate. I am one of the Aqrab." To Beaux the word sounded like "ak-rawb."

"It is a Hebrew word which translates to scorpion. A scorpion may be the insect or when used figuratively, a scourge or knotted whip," Friedman explained. "In the Hebrew and Christian Bible there are the books of Kings and Chronicles. Within them it is said, 'I will discipline or chastise you with scorpions' and 'I will discipline you with whips.' Whips... scorpions... Aqrab; this is where the name of our group comes from."

"Why have I never heard of your group?" Delys asked.

Friedman smiled, "We are not what you'd call... a well known entity; we seek neither acknowledgement nor accolades. We are deadly serious in our mission. We concern ourselves with beginnings and endings; we are unafraid of either and embrace both conditions. We are curious and quite adept investigators. We are also personally committed, very much like the scorpion; we would rather kill ourselves than be killed. Also, we have tremendous regenerative powers; much like the literal scorpion can lose its tail and promptly grow a new one—each of us is expendable. When one of us falls, another takes his place. We will not lose; we just keep on going. We have a focus, protection not necessarily of the individual but the essence of the Jewish faith."

"We have learned that survival of an individual is tied directly to the survival of our beliefs and customs. When an individual is essential to the survival of those, the survival of that individual is essential to us. We have learned that nothing is ever truly safe; nothing is immortal... except what we leave behind us. And in truth, even those may be transitory."

"Because we are stubborn and determined to succeed, our people are intense, passionate, and filled with desire. Our organization is both complex and simple; we were formed during the holocaust and remain alive even today because we are secretive. We are surprisingly resourceful and suspicious. It is best not to bet against us."

Friedman paused, puffing on the pipe, "Frankly, most of the people we have introduced ourselves to... well, let us say they have not been in the position to talk about us after the meetings." Beaux moved suddenly, whipping his hand behind his back snatching the little .38 and thumbing the hammer back to full cock.

"Mr. Friedman," Beaux said coolly, "provided you and your men do not move we can continue this pleasant conversation. However, I would advise you of several things. Number one, I prefer friendly conversations to be that... friendly. Should you wish to contact me again, this is not the method I would use. Number two, your search for weapons sucked. Friendly advice, don't stop when you find a gun... look for a backup. Number three, direct your driver to pull to the side of the road, slowly please."

Friedman looked at the revolver, "Mr. Delys, really... a pearl handled revolver. Isn't that a bit ostentatious?"

Beaux smiled, "To paraphrase George Patton, 'They're ivory. Only a pimp from a cheap whorehouse would carry a pearl-handled pistol.'" Then he tilted the revolver's barrel up, eased the hammer down with his thumb and put it back in the holster. "Now Aharon, what is all of this about?"

Chapter Thirty-One

Charles Fredricks' restored 1961 Cessna Skyhawk climbed slowly into the night sky after departing Kaanapali Airport for a night flight from the west coast of Maui to the old abandoned Kipapa Field on Oahu—a distance of only about ninety miles. His passenger sat quietly holding a package in his lap. Fredricks didn't know the man's name and frankly didn't want to. The college professor was paying off a debt. Fredricks had a problem, he was being blackmailed; he should have known better. *How could I have been so stupid?* he thought. *I should have seen this coming.*

The first contact had come over his cell phone and it seemed innocent enough. The teenage sister of a former student had texted asking for guidance on decisions regarding college. It wasn't long before the texts developed a romantic twist. That first meeting had been incredible, intoxicating and Fredricks was hooked. The second and third meetings followed within days and his life started spiraling. The hook was set; photos began arriving at his office.

He tried to break it off but it was too late. Then the phone call came followed by the first meeting with the blackmailer; it wasn't long before a financial crisis was reached and the first of several flights had started. By then he had drained his retirement funds and just as he was sinking under the weight, he had been given a promise of being able to replenish his retirement funds with the assurance that his "dalliance" would not go public.

He only had two more flights after this one before it ended; at least that was what he had been promised. Each flight had been made in darkness without a flight plan being filed and at low altitude over the ocean to avoid radar detection. He shook his head thinking, *a drowning man will grab at any straw.* He refocused on his control panel when a low level beep sounded in his headphone. *Hmmm, everything seems okay.*

He checked his collision alert system. The latest generation of the FLARM, or "flight alarm," could detect potential airborne targets within three to five kilometers. Motion-prediction algorithms predict potential hazards and warn the pilot using sound and visual signals. *Something is out there,* he thought as he visually scanned the night sky. *Don't see it yet.*

Whatever it was seemed to be approaching off his left wing; he reached down for the night vision goggles and put them on.

"Anything wrong?" the passenger asked.

Fredricks was scanning the sky intently, "I don't think so, probably a flight of birds." While some birds did fly and some species even migrate at night, he had never encountered it himself, at least not over the open ocean at this altitude.

His passenger looked out the windscreen, "I don't see anything."

"Me either," Fredricks said. Then something splattered on the windscreen; the splats increased. Fredricks shouted, "What the..." just as the windscreen suddenly disintegrated. Hundreds, if not thousands, of small bodies slammed into the men. The passenger screamed, "Bugs, stinging bugs..." then he was silent. Many bugs had died on impact, the others slammed into the men with stinging barbs flashing into their skin and clothing; the pain was incredible and the damage was immediate and devastating. The Skyhawk nosed down even as Fredricks struggled to pull up; he couldn't.

The Skyhawk's fuselage crumbled on impact with the water to less than a third of its twenty-seven foot length and the wings ripped off. In seconds, the plane, pilot, and passenger disappeared below the waves. There was no surface debris, just a light skim of fuel. The swarm of large insects continued on its path.

Chapter Thirty-Two

Rourke answered his cell phone with a distracted, "Hello."

"Hello Dr. Rourke, my name is William Kirby, I'm an entomologist."

"You study bugs, right? What can I do for you?"

"Yes, I study bugs," Kirby said. "But I think there is something I can do for you. We entomologists help farmers and ranchers produce crops and livestock more efficiently by developing pest management strategies, providing information on endangered species, and some of the fragile ecosystems that make up our environment. We help to prevent the spread of serious diseases in plants and animals."

Rourke nodded to himself, "Just out of curiosity, how did you get into that business?"

"Well, honestly, as a kid I liked bugs," Kirby said smiling at the phone. "I was naturally curious and drawn to puzzles and problem-solving not to mention science. Seemed to me like a natural fit. Anyway, the reason I'm calling is I believe we have a problem. A county extension director found an insect about a week, maybe ten days ago near the site of a cluster of reports of illness and several deaths on one of the neighboring islands. He had never seen anything like this and thought it may be related. He was correct and I can tell you that without a doubt, this is a terrorist attack."

Rourke frowned, "How can you be so sure? If people are sick and you found the carrier, why can it not be a natural disease?"

Kirby said seriously, "The disease is, the carrier is not. This insect doesn't exist it nature, it has been genetically engineered. Bear with me; this is going to get rather complicated. As near as I can tell, this carrier probably started as a Dryococelus australis, more commonly known as the Lord Howe Island stick insect or tree lobster. That is a species of stick insect thought to be extinct by 1930—that is until 1964 when a dead one was discovered on a neighboring island fourteen miles away. Several more dead insects were discovered later, but a live one wasn't found until much later."

"These insects can measure up to 5.9 inches in length and weigh just less than an ounce, with females bigger than males. They are oblong in shape and have sturdy legs and they are flightless. Males have thicker thighs than females. The behavior of this stick insect is highly unusual for an insect species. The males and females form a bond; the males follow the females and their activities depend on what the female is doing. Females lay eggs while hanging from branches and the eggs hatch up to nine months later. They are nocturnal. Normally these insects have no wings, but are able to run quickly. These new ones have wings... and also carry the DNA of the Melanoplus bruneri."

"What the hell is that?" Rourke asked.

"The Rocky Mountain locust," Kirby said as he stretched his back which was hurting from hours over a microscope. "They have had some of the largest recorded swarms in history, and were supposed to have died out in the late nineteenth century. We have confirmed that in this subject specimen there are actually three separate and identifiable DNA genomes, from three separate and distinct species. This level of genetic splicing from three different species is beyond anything I have ever seen. This third DNA strand is linked to a very nasty creature; the venomous scorpion. All scorpions have a tail that delivers venom. Most will only give a human victim a bad few days, but 25 of the over 1,000 known species can kill a person."

Rourke shook his head, "And this vector has the DNA of all three. How in the world is such a creature possible?"

"Like I said in the beginning, in this world it is not possible. This new creature was created artificially with some very extreme and advanced genetic manipulation—manipulation far beyond our technology. Luckily, the three different species have one thing in common; all three prefer to nest underground in burrows. This new beastie does also. It is the carrier or vector for this new epidemic and it was created artificially and on purpose. That is why I say this is a terrorist attack."

Rourke asked, "How do we kill them? And by the way, what are you calling it?"

"On an individual scale, step on 'em; provided you're wearing shoes. Change that to boots... heavy boots, this thing is dangerous. I'm not sure how to handle a population density this size, but we have to solve that question fast. We were able to find twenty-five specimens. What we have learned is they have an extremely high reproductive rate and we haven't found a natural or artificial poison that works. For right now, we're calling it a VBB. If we don't destroy these hosts quickly..." he hesitated.

Rourke filled in the blank, "They will destroy us. Okay give me your address." He copied the address onto a scrap of paper. Rourke thought for a moment, "I can be there in about thirty minutes. By the way, VBB, is that some kind of scientific designation; what does it stand for?"

"No, we haven't decided on a scientific name. In the lab we're just calling it a Very Bad Bug," Kirby said with a wry smile and broke the connection.

Chapter Thirty-Three

John pulled into the parking lot and noticed a black sedan with Medical Examiner on the door. He walked into the lobby and to a wall directory, finding the number for Kirby's office on the third floor. A short elevator ride later, he entered Kirby's office and found two men. "I'm here to see Mr. Kirby, I'm John Rourke."

Kirby stood and they shook hands. "This is Dr. Stevens, the County Medical Examiner. I've already briefed him."

"Okay Doc." Rourke turned to the medical doctor. "What exactly is this about?"

"A genetically modified hantavirus or HPS," Dr. Stevens said.

Rourke thought for a moment, "Wait a minute; if I am remembering my epidemiology classes correctly, the Hantavirus is transmitted by rodent urine, rodent droppings, and saliva of infected rodents, not bugs."

Stevens nodded, "You are correct. Early symptoms include fatigue, fever, and muscle aches, especially in the large muscle groups... thighs, hips, back, and sometimes shoulders. These symptoms are universal. There may also be headaches, dizziness, chills, and abdominal problems, such as nausea, vomiting, diarrhea, and abdominal pain. Four to ten days after the initial phase of illness, the late symptoms of HPS appear. These include coughing and shortness of breath, with the sensation of, as one survivor put it, a 'tight band around my chest and a pillow over my face' as the lungs fill with fluid."

"The old strains could be fatal, right?" Rourke asked.

"Yes, a mortality rate of thirty-nine percent," Kirby said; Stevens nodded his head in agreement.

"It is a serious infection that gets worse quickly. Lung failure can occur and may lead to death. Even with aggressive treatment, more than half of the people who have this disease in their lungs die."

"Are you saying this strain is different?" Rourke asked.

Stevens nodded, "Yes, much more virulent and aggressive. The symptoms can start in as little as a few hours from original exposure. Most deaths, as near as we can tell, are occurring within twenty-four to thirty-six hours after exposure."

Rourke thought for a moment and said, "Alright, you're telling me this is being spread by these VBBs. Do you know where they came from or where they first appeared?"

Kirby walked to a map and pointed to one of the smaller islands in the Hawaiian chain. "We are not absolutely positive but right now we think they first appeared somewhere in this area."

John frowned, "Are you absolutely sure about the rest of this information?" Both nodded. Rourke continued, "I mean are you 100 percent sure of these facts, will they stand scrutiny by the highest authorities?" Again both nodded. Rourke wiped his face with both hands, "Okay, may I borrow your phone?" Kirby slid the phone across the table; Rourke picked up the hand piece and dialed Michael's private number.

"Hello..."

"Michael, we have to talk, now. I've got two gentlemen who you need to hear from."

Chapter Thirty-Four

Rain was falling slowly as Darrel Jackson crawled into his shelter; a discarded cardboard shipping container covered by a piece of plastic sheeting taped into place. Inside was a small discarded mattress he had found along the street; it was his only degree of cushioning from the cold, hard concrete beneath him. A spasm of coughing erupted as he rearranged the filthy blankets that smelled as bad as he did. For days he had been hacking up dark globs of yellow/green phylum from his lungs. He reached inside the old field jacket and removed his only companion; an ugly, small, mixed breed puppy he had found wandering in the alley. Darrel lay down and the pup squirmed close for warmth next to his chest.

His life was not supposed to turn out like this, but it had. Bad decisions, drugs, alcohol, and gambling debts had reduced him from a young successful business man with a college degree, to a homeless bum eking out an existence on the streets. He had lost it all—wife, kids and a future. Destitute didn't cover the malaise and squalor of his life any more than misery described his loneliness.

The puppy looked up and gave Darrell a lick on the nose. Smiling, Darrell petted the pup and said softly, "Ah, puppy breath, the magic elixir." Suddenly, he felt a sharp stinging pain in his right leg, just above the worn out ankle boots he had found last week. He hollered, "Son of a bitch..." as he slapped at the pain. "Damn, that hurts," he told the puppy. Pulling up his pants leg he saw his attacker, "What the hell... a damn scorpion!"

His attacker was not killed by the impact, the bug kept stabbing its stinger into the man's leg. "Crap!" he shouted as he struck again with no effect. He grabbed the scorpion and ripped it from his leg throwing it across the alley way. It struck the brick wall and fell to the ground and crawled off. "Damn son of a bitching bug, must have hit me six times," he told the puppy while rubbing his injured leg. He pulled the pup closer and the two settled down; the pup was shivering. The man snored deeply and sweated.

Had he been awake, he might have heard the humming of wings approaching during the night; he didn't. The scorpion had returned with reinforcements; sixteen of them landed close to the man's shelter. Almost as though they had a plan in mind, the aggressive predators silently moved inside the shelter and up the man's pant leg. They stung him again and again before they crawled off looking for another victim; but the man didn't react.

Thirty minutes later, the coughing returned. His immune system, almost ten years of a lifestyle fraught with drugs and malnutrition, was unable to fight off the venom from the stings. Less than an hour later, the man, unconscious rather than asleep, choked on several massive globs of phylum his labored lungs expelled, and died.

The pup, unharmed and unaware of the attack, slept on. Finally, he stirred. He was cold and something was wrong with the man. There was no heat coming from him. The puppy stayed until the rain quit and crawled from the dead man's grip, turned and gave a last lick to the man's cold dead face and left to find another benefactor.

It was three days later before someone noticed the stench coming from the cardboard box and called the city sanitation department. The two city workers gagged as they pulled the container down and looked at the bloated body. "I ain't touching this," one said as he pulled his radio. "Yeah, Central, this is McClannahan. We have a dead body here, better notify the Coroner." The radio crackled, McClannahan said, "No, looks natural. Homeless guy; been dead for a while. Get a wagon down here to pick him up."

Chapter Thirty-Five

Two hours later, three men approached the Secret Service agent at the gate of the presidential mansion. After checking their identification he said, "The President is expecting you." Ten minutes later, they were sitting in the small conference room in the west wing. Dr. Stevens was laying out the reports when the President, Michael Rourke, entered.

Walking over to his father Michael said, "Dad, I only have a few minutes. I hope this is important, my calendar is pretty full."

John nodded, "Son, you are probably going to have to clear it. I suggest you call in the head of the CDC and the head of the National Security Agency. At least have them standing by on a secure phone line to listen to this. We have a problem."

Michael looked at his father, "Let me hear it first, then I'll make those arrangements if it is necessary." Thirty minutes into the presentation Michael punched the call button on the intercom and a Marine guard knocked on the door and entered. Michael rose from the table and handed a note to the guard, "Take this to the Chief of Staff and tell him I want a secure phone line set up immediately with the first person on this list. Tell him to contact the others and get them over here right now."

The Marine saluted, about faced and marched out the door. Michael turned back and looked at the three men sadly. "Gentlemen, on one hand I hope you know what you're talking about. On the other hand, I pray you don't. In either event, that is about to be determined." He checked his watch, "We probably have about thirty minutes before we start again. I'd suggest you may want to take a bathroom break; if what you're telling me is accurate, it will be a while before you get another. I have to adjust my schedule. I'll be back in about twenty minutes."

Michael walked into his personal office. After calling his secretary to clear his calendar he dialed another number. Several short beeps sounded in the ear piece; Michael spoke the activation code, "Lockout, Papa Baker," and hung up.

Chapter Thirty-Six

The Marine guard knocked on the door to the small conference room and entered, "Gentlemen, the President has asked for you to follow me to another location." Kirby and Stevens gathered their information and followed John Rourke and the Marine down the hall to the elevator. They descended three levels below into the ground. *We're going to the War Room*, Rourke thought. He was correct.

When they entered, Michael directed them to chairs at the large conference table. As the last man entered, Michael told the Marine guard, "Unless there is a national security matter of the highest order, we are not to be disturbed." The Marine saluted and went to parade rest.

Michael closed the door, went to his seat and punched a button on a large speaker box on the conference table. "Dan, can you hear us alright?"

Dan Hasher of the Lock Out Team said, "Yes, Mr. President, I can."

Michael introduced the Director of the National Security Agency, Harmon Knowles who turned and introduced his Deputy Director of Intelligence, Darrell Cooper and the Deputy Director of Operations, Dave Sheppard.

Michael turned to his father, "Dad, let's get this started."

John Rourke nodded, introduced Kirby and Stevens and said, "These gentlemen have a story you need to hear. They are saying we have been attacked... we don't know by whom, but they believe they have identified the what and the how."

"Hold it," NSA Director Knowles interrupted, looking at his two subordinates who shook their heads, "Attacked? I have no word of any attack."

John nodded, "That sir is the problem. Dr. Stevens and Mr. Kirby have indications that the attack has already begun and we have been targeted by a genetically engineered biological threat. Mr. Kirby, please tell them what you told me and the President."

Kirby cleared his throat as he passed out a series of photographs. "This is what I know right now..." He began.

When he was finished, he turned to Dr. Stevens, "Your turn Doc." His briefing was short and not very news worthy.

Chapter Thirty-Seven

That evening, as Michael and Natalia sat alone in her hospital room, he asked, "What do you know about Russian development of biological weapons?"

She thought for a long moment, going back through memories from before the Night of the War. "I know that the Soviet Union began a BW program in the 1920s although they were a signatory to the 1925 Geneva Protocol, which banned both chemical and biological weapons. During the second World War, Stalin had moved his biological operations out of the path of advancing German forces and may have used tularemia against German troops in 1942 near Stalingrad."

"By 1960, numerous BW research facilities existed throughout the Soviet Union. Although the USSR also signed the 1972 Biological Weapons Convention, the Soviets subsequently augmented their biological warfare programs. Over the course of its history, the Soviet program is known to have weaponized and stockpiled the several bio-agents and pursued basic research on many more."

"These programs became immense and were conducted at 52 clandestine sites employing over 50,000 people. Annualized production capacity for weaponized smallpox, for example, was 90 to 100 tons. In the 1980s, many of these agents were genetically altered to resist heat, cold, and antibiotics. We know that a scientist named Igor Domaradskij and Colonel Kanatjan Alibekov, who both defected, were in charge of several of these operations. Alibekov admitted a biological weapons accident in 1979 had resulted in the deaths of at least 64 people. Another outbreak of weaponized smallpox had occurred earlier during testing in 1971. There was a professor..." Natalia said, frustrated and unable to remember his name, "Damn, my head hurts."

"Do you need to rest?" Michael asked, concerned.

"No, it's on the tip of my tongue... Burgasov, that's his name, Burgasov. Hand me your phone Michael, I need to search something." She typed into a search engine. "Here it is; a report from General Professor Peter Burgasov, former Chief Sanitary Physician of the Soviet Army, and a senior researcher within the program of biological weapons. Let me read this to you; it's a report he wrote on an incident he witnessed."

"'On Vozrozhdeniya Island in the Aral Sea, the strongest formulations of smallpox were tested. Suddenly, I was informed that there were mysterious cases of mortalities in Aralsk. A research ship of the Aral fleet had come within fifteen kilometers from the island, it was forbidden for anyone else to come any closer than forty kilometers. The lab technician of this ship took samples of plankton twice a day from the top deck.'"

"'The smallpox formulation, 400 grams of which was exploded on the island got her, and she became infected. After returning home to Aralsk, she infected several people, including children. All of them died. I suspected the reason for this and called the General Chief of Staff at the Ministry of Defense and requested to forbid the Alma-Ata train from stopping in Aralsk. As a result, an epidemic throughout the country was prevented. I called Andropov, who at that time was the Chief of the KGB, and informed him of the unique formulation of smallpox obtained on Vozrozhdeniya Island.'"

"I personally know," Natalia said, handing Michael his phone, "that by the Night of the War the program had been massive and still existed. An agreement was signed with the US and UK promising to end bio-weapons programs and convert BW facilities to benevolent purposes, but compliance with the agreement—and the fate of the former Soviet bio-agents and facilities—is still mostly undocumented."

"We think," Michael said, "someone named Yuri Burgasov is the bad guy. His grandfather, several times removed, died of Marburg virus disease."

"The Marburg virus's name is derived from Marburg, where the virus was first discovered. It is a hemorrhagic fever virus first noticed and described during small epidemics when workers were accidentally exposed to Chlorocebus aethiops, at the city's former main industrial plant—the Behringwerke, then part of Hoechst. During these outbreaks, if I remember correctly, thirty-one people became infected and seven of them died. Marburg virus, or MARV, causes severe disease in humans and nonhuman primates in the form of viral hemorrhagic fever. Marburg virus was first described somewhere around 1967."

Chapter Thirty-Eight

"Paul, we need to talk in person," John Rourke said into the phone. Paul had been released from medical care except for the cast on his leg. He'd be wheeling around in a wheelchair for the next several weeks—his mobility was limited. "Are you feeling up to a visitor, can I come over?"

"Sure."

"Good, do me a favor and call your pal, that emergency services guy you know," John said.

"Randal Walls?"

"Yeah, that's his name. Ask him if I can pick him up on my way over. If there's a problem, let me know. Do you have his address? Also, give him a high-level heads-up about the bugs so he'll know what this is about."

Paul gave Rourke the address and called Walls to let him know John was on his way. Forty minutes later, Rourke and Walls knocked on Paul's front door. "Thanks for having us, Paul. Randall," John said, "I need to pick your brain." They walked into Paul's study as he wheeled in behind them. Annie came in and gave her dad a hug. "Can I get you gentlemen anything?"

"No Honey, we'll just be a minute," John said. Annie kissed Paul and tossed a "If you change your minds..." over her shoulder. Rourke explained what he could about the threat. Finally, John asked, "So, what do you think, Randall?"

Walls scratched his head, "Well, if you are correct, this is not going to be simple. You're talking about searching almost 6,500 square miles. Remember, in addition to the eight main islands—Hawaii, Maui, Kahoolawe, Lanai, Molokai, Oahu, Kauai, and Niihau—there are 152 separate islands listed in the Hawaiian chain. These include smaller island chains such as the French Frigate Shoals, which includes thirteen islands of its own."

"This list didn't number the uninhabited islets, rocks, coral reefs, and atolls. On Oahu alone, it would be necessary to activate at least twenty-eight local agencies in response to such an outbreak. Those would include the Capital City Fire and Police Departments, County Sheriff's Offices and School Districts,

County Health Departments, Air Quality, and Emergency Management, just to mention a few. Add to that mix the Red Cross, pharmacies, Medical Examiners, Hospitals, and the rest; it adds up pretty quickly."

"What about on the national level?" Rubenstein asked.

Walls said, "Those numbers don't even come close to addressing the numbers related to the national level if the outbreak went to the epidemic level. Looking at the possibility of a global pandemic, the word 'daunting' doesn't come close to describing the situation. In that event, the level of coordination, not to mention implementation of recovery and mediation activities, has never been designed; much less practiced. There simply has not been such an outbreak since the Dark Ages when bubonic plague wiped out over a third of the population of Europe. That had also been a vector borne disease—rats. Rats couldn't fly; you're saying this vector can."

"If we have a full blown outbreak, it's going to be messy." Walls pulled a brochure from his coat pocket and gave it to John. "This example will show you how we need to respond. It's a synopsis of the first of three modules for the actions at the Emergency Operations Center on day one of the full-scale exercise. Similar plans are included for each element of play to include public information and rumor control. Players have to consider the availability and adequacy of local and state medical supplies to treat the epidemic and discuss how the Governor's Office would make state-level assistance available to the affected counties. Finally, the players acknowledge that quarantine measures would have to be considered."

Chapter Thirty-Nine

The CEO of Lancer Firearms, Daniel Ferguson, was new to his position but he and Rourke had met on several occasions. "Here's what I'm going to need," Rourke told him, "and this has to be an off-the-books project for reasons I can't discuss. Agreed?"

"Sure John. Lancer doesn't need to know why you need something. We just need to know what it is and then see if we can make it. You're calling this contraption a flamethrower. From your layout I can guess what it does, but how does the damn thing work?"

"The flamethrower consists of two primary elements: a pressurized fuel source and the gun. On a man-portable version, the fuel source is located in a backpack element that usually consists of two or three cylinders. In a two-cylinder system, one cylinder holds compressed, inert propellant gas, usually nitrogen, and the other holds flammable liquid—typically gasoline with some form of fuel thickener added to it. A three-cylinder system often has two outer cylinders of flammable liquid and a central cylinder of propellant gas."

"The gas propels the liquid fuel out of the cylinder through a flexible pipe and then into the gun element of the flamethrower system. The gun consists of a small reservoir, a spring-loaded valve, and an ignition system. Depressing a trigger opens the valve, allowing pressurized flammable liquid to flow and pass over the igniter and out of the gun nozzle. The igniter can be one of several ignition systems. A simple type is an electrically-heated wire coil. Another used is a small pilot flame, fueled with pressurized gas from the system."

"They were primarily used against battlefield fortifications, bunkers, caves, and other protected emplacements. The old flamethrower projected a stream of flammable liquid, rather than flame, which allows bouncing the stream off walls and ceilings of an enclosure. Typically, flamethrowers can incinerate a target at a distance between 165 to 270 feet."

"I know that the concept of throwing fire as a weapon has existed since ancient times," Ferguson said. "Early flame weapons date from the Byzantine era;

these were rudimentary hand-pumped flamethrowers on naval vessels in the early first century AD."

"Correct," Rourke said. "The Germans invented the first flamethrower, in the modern sense. Our word 'flamethrower' comes from the German word, Flammenwerfer. That one saw service during the First World War. Improvements were made because that one shot a jet of fire and enormous clouds of smoke but only about twenty yards and it was a single-shot weapon. By the time the Second World War came along, significant improvements were made and they saw service in every theater of operations. The Soviets even went so far as to camouflage their flamethrowers. The ROKS-2 was disguised as a standard issue rifle and the fuel tanks as a standard infantryman's rucksack, to try to stop snipers from specifically targeting flamethrower operators."

"What range do you want this thing to have and how many do you need?"

"As much as you can push out of them. As soon as we have a working prototype we will need at least thirty. We want a man-portable version with a range of several hundred feet at least. We also want one that can be vehicle mounted; that one needs to have some real range and, since it's on a vehicle, a man won't have to haul the weight. If they work as planned, this could be a major deal for Lancer. There could be a global application because these things were outlawed years ago and you will be the only source."

"John," Ferguson said, "you know while Lancer is in business to make money, our primary focus has always been service—especially to you and your family and certainly our own government."

"I know that," Rourke said. "Your company has always been discrete and what you create is the equal of any product I've ever seen. When do you think you can have a working prototype to test?"

"Damn thing doesn't appear to be very complex. Honestly, that's what scares me. When something seems simple and easy, it generally isn't. I can see this being extremely dangerous, not only on the business end of the nozzle but for the guy carrying it. I want to really test our theories—that is as soon as we develop some—before we go into full scale production. Let me get my design team on this and figure out how to do it. Give me two days to 'noodle' it and we can talk. Is that acceptable?"

*****

Eighteen hours later, Rourke grabbed his phone on the second ring, "Hello."

"John." Rourke recognized Ferguson's voice.

"Yes, Daniel."

"Can you get over to Lancer? I've got something to show you."

"Already?" Rourke asked. "I didn't expect to hear from you until tomorrow."

"Yes, my engineer came up with an idea. I want you to see it first before we go any further."

Rourke looked at his Rolex, "Give me twenty minutes?"

"Fine, come on."

Chapter Forty

"John, we ran into a couple of problems straight away," Ferguson said. "But I think we have found a 'work-around.' If you agree to it, it will cut weeks off of production. You said this was a rush order, right?"

"That's right," Rourke said. "Time is definitely of the essence. Show me."

Ferguson said, "Follow me out back." They went through the production floor and out the rear of the building to the firing range where they tested new ideas. "John, this is Jim Downey, my head engineer."

"Mr. Rourke," Downey said as they shook hands. "It's a pleasure to finally meet you."

"What have you got Jim? Daniel said you encountered some problems."

Downey nodded, "Not serious problems, your design was simple enough from a mechanical point of view. The problem was the time frame. It would take us weeks to refit our production line just to come up with a prototype. However; I think this will work just as well and it is a lot quicker to construct." He pulled out what appeared to be a standard energy rifle from its case.

Rourke shook his head, "This won't work guys, we need flame and heat on a wider scale than this produces. A blast from this energy rifle is going to be too focused. We need to kill the vector in numbers of thousands, not one at a time."

Downey nodded, "Hold on a second and watch this..." He turned the activation switch on and made some adjustments. A stream of green fire erupted in an arch from the muzzle; it traveled almost 100 feet before igniting a stack of wooden pallets. Flames shot skyward.

"Damn," Rourke said. "What was that?"

Downy said, "Standard energy rifle but I made a module that is a frequency modulator. You know the standard energy weapon sends an individual bolt of high energy down range. That bolt of high energy is comprised of modulated plasma, modulated and set at very high range. That setting is necessary for down range accuracy, almost at a pin point level. That was what was so time consuming in the original design; how it functioned. Originally, all the designers could get, is exactly what we're trying to make happen now."

"We knew that wouldn't work for your application. Fortunately, we were able to just go back and reengineer the 'problem' the original designers had to overcome. In the beginning, they struggled with how to increase the 'flow' of energy to a 'usable projectile' of energy. Understand?"

Rourke nodded, "You're saying they started with a flow and improved it to a pulse?"

Downy nodded. "Exactly, they had the reverse of what you wanted. With this frequency modulator, I have reduced those individual bolts of high energy back to a stream of lower energy plasma; lower energy but higher temperature. That means instead of single bolts of high energy, the weapons is capable of generating a continuous stream of energy of high temperature plasma. You don't have the long range accuracy or the impact devastation, but you have blistering heat, approaching 2,000 degrees that can be sprayed like a stream of water."

"Won't that melt the barrel pretty quickly?" Rourke asked.

"Watch again," Downey said as he aimed and pulled the trigger.

"Got it," Rourke nodded. "The fire doesn't start until the steam has already left the barrel."

"Exactly," Downey said as he safed the weapon. "Two, two and a half feet after it leaves the barrel. The weapon and the operator are not exposed to the high temperature. Additionally, this is a quick fix. Rather than create a new weapon, which would take weeks for that many units, we just modify this one and the modifications only take about an hour per weapon."

"Do you have all the parts? I mean how long would it take to have twenty to thirty ready to go?"

"Yes, we do," Ferguson said, "and we can have you thirty functional in... two days, if we go around the clock. Then it is only a question of making more out of something that already exists."

Rourke nodded, "Daniel, make it happen. You're sure there's no danger for the operator?"

"No more so than normal and this is a proven design with proven technology. All we're really doing..." He paused, coming up with the proper analogy. "We're not changing ammo so to speak, just how it functions."

"How about the capacity, how long will one weapon function if it starts out fully charged?"

Downy thought, "On continuous stream, probably fifteen minutes. If the operator uses short, controlled streams—double that. Plus, the same energy pack currently in use to power the energy rifle is used to reload; that just takes a few seconds and you're back at full charge, ready to start over again. The good news is we don't have to waste time on research and development. I mean, we don't have to fabricate or recreate a weapon that none of us are familiar with or have any experience with. This design also eliminates the bulky and heavy fuel backpack completely, plus the nozzle and igniter contraption from your design. It only increases the normal weight of the weapon by about 1.5 ounces. Plus, it will eliminate the time involved in training people to safely operate your design. If you can spray a water hose, you can operate this weapon. Lastly, all we have to do is remove the modulator and the weapon returns to its normal functioning. That can be done in the field by the operator, without any special tools and only about ten minutes of training."

Chapter Forty-One

Akiro Kuriname's successful "transition" had opened the possibilities for the clones, during the tunnel sweep, to salvage their lives. If Kuriname could be saved, logic said that maybe the others could be as well. The attempt was made. Those housed at the Ambrose Federal Detention Center had been hit with oneirogenic general anesthetic, the formal name for sleeping gas; it was pumped into the cell blocks, rendering them unconscious. Once the atmosphere had been purged, the unconscious prisoners had been transferred to the main gymnasium area where four "operating tents" stood; within each was a surgery team that worked in relays.

The removal of all of the alien tattoos took less than three hours. Once removed each tissue sample had been placed in stasis for later study and analysis. Now, three weeks later, Dr. David Blackman, Chief of Psychological Research at Mid-Wake and Dr. Henry Drake, Chief of Medicine at Tripler were ready to enter the second phase of the prisoners "reconditioning." Blackman said, "Luckily, Rourke's theory proved to be correct. Our assumption is that when Akiro Kuriname was knocked unconscious, the link between he and the aliens was temporally broken; and, since the tattoo was removed prior to his regaining consciousness, it has been severed completely."

Drake nodded, "David, we still are not sure how the tattoo linkage works. The best we can come up with right now is there is some method of biochemical interaction with... I don't know. The closest analogy would be something like nanotechnology present in the tissues. Frankly, we haven't seen anything like this before; I just can't explain how it works."

"That is something," Blackman said, taking a sip of hot green tea. Blackman's favorite tea was a Moroccan Mint loose leaf blend. The mixture of traditional Marrakech Gunpowder tea, peppermint, and spearmint gave a smooth flavor. The Green Gunpowder base was subtly sweet without the normal bite of the mint. Properly prepared—brewed at 180 degrees Fahrenheit and steeped for three minutes, then re-steeped twice more—it was a relaxing beverage that he thought was equally delicious when iced. It was his single passion, almost a vice.

"That is something we will simply have to continue researching. It is relevant certainly, but the important issue is we have been able to break that linkage. Psychologically, these men are 'rescued.' Henry, I'm ready to proceed. Is there any reason, any medical reason, you see for further delays?"

Drake shook his head, he drank a simple but strong cup of coffee; black. "No, the syn-skin grafts have all healed. Medically, they are healthy. I am however, still concerned by how well they have rehabilitated emotionally. I have concern about using these men as Guinea pigs."

"I know Henry," Blackman said nodding. "But as Rourke stated, if we had not been successful they would have spent the rest of their lives as prisoners. We wouldn't have had a choice; now these men can at least see the light of day as free citizens. I say it's time to move forward."

"Then let's bring in Mr. Kuriname and get started."

Chapter Forty-Two

The main gymnasium area of the Ambrose Federal Detention Center was quiet, deafeningly so. Thirty-four men wearing white hospital scrubs sat on metal folding chairs, unmoving and facing the speaker's podium. Chairs were set up between two large white boards and several flip charts along the north wall. Along the south wall, Wes Sanderson's men sat at the position of attention. A door opened behind them and the clip clop of heels striking the concrete floor echoed through the room, yet not one turned to see who was approaching.

Akiro Kuriname walked around the group, followed by Doctors Blackman and Drake, John Thomas Rourke and Wes Sanderson. They joined newly appointed Brigadier General Rodney Thorne and General Sullivan on stage. Kuriname went to the podium as the others took their seats behind him. He laid a manila folder on the speaker's stand, opened it, cleared his throat and raised his eyes to look at the men.

"Good morning," Kuriname said with a slight bow. "I'm going to make this a short presentation today. I have been authorized to make you an offer. I have had the opportunity to discuss the potentiality of this offer with several of you; those I have talked to have understood the significance of the offer and now it is time for a decision to be made. I, like you, have been violated—physically, emotionally and... yes, if I may say so... spiritually. The people we are... and we are truly people, are a reflection of our 'originals' or parents, if you will."

"Like you, I am still trying to define..." He stopped for a moment and scanned the faces. "To define, what I am. Most important to that process has been to define the 'who' I wish to be. The shock of realization has now been replaced with a sense of purpose and to a degree, a sense of anger and need for justice. Before, in that world that existed so long ago, people were chosen for an incredible mission. A mission, it was hoped, could salvage mankind from its own stupidity. Our Parents, it is said, 'were the best, the brightest and bravest' America could find. Rather, I would say, they were simply 'the chosen' who America sent."

Dr. Blackman stirred a little in his seat but said nothing. "America chose them for that mission; circumstances have chosen us for another," Kuriname said. "I will now introduce my friend, in fact, the man who saved me, Doctor General John Rourke. I would like to add he is responsible for saving each of you from the life we were created for. John," he said and turned the meeting over to Rourke.

Rourke stood and went to one of the white boards as Akiro took his seat. "As far back into history as you want to go, specialized units operating as 'guerrillas' were able to accomplish what larger armies could not. They operated behind the lines, in secret and in constant danger. They were silent heroes of the highest order. You have the opportunity to be part of such a unit. Based on your 'unique' status, you possess all that remains of training and experiences gained by your fathers during their training for the Eden Project. That knowledge will be essential for this project. Anyone interested? If so, please stand."

The scraping of thirty-four metal chairs sliding on the concrete floor sounded as one as thirty-four men stood silently at the position of attention. "Good, it is time for some pay back," Rourke said. Each of you constitutes a life yet to be lived. You have a blank slate to work with. Whereas you had zero control a few weeks ago, you are in absolute control of your futures. That said, it will be up to you to define that life. By conventional standards, you don't exist; but you do. You are unencumbered by families or past performance."

"By society's standards, you might as well be dead. Your parents, as Akiro calls them, each had to leave a life for their mission. Lives, families, careers... all of that; you on the other hand have the chance to create those things. Your mission is to bring those qualities and abilities your parents had to the foreground; and in doing that you will become the best, the brightest, and bravest America could find this go around. Instead of being chosen, you are choosing; it is a subtle but significant difference."

Rourke took a deep breath and glanced at a note card, "To paraphrase Thomas Paine, 'It seems we are poised and have every opportunity and every encouragement before us, to form the noblest purest constitution on the face of the Earth. We have it in our power to begin the world over again. A situation, similar to the present, hath not happened since the days of Noah until now. The birthday of a new world is at hand and a race of men, perhaps all this planet contains, are about to receive their portion of freedom.' I'm going to turn the meeting back over to Lieutenant Kuriname; excuse me, it's Lieutenant Commander Kuriname, who will conduct the rest of your briefing."

Akiro divided the group into three ten-man squads, with an officer team leader for each and a Non Commissioned Officer to be shared by all three. The NCO was to function as the group's collective First Sergeant. "Each of you has experience as members of an elite light infantry or special operations force with specialized training. You form the second element of this team. This will be a joint operation; a tightly coordinated strike force whose mission is still being defined. You will be assigned to pair up with one of Chief Sanderson's men. They will train you in the 'finer' aspect of Close Quarters Combat and weapons training. I will brief you on the details after this meeting. Team Leader for Alpha Team, after that briefing, you will take your folks for your final medical evaluation."

Chapter Forty-Three

Later that evening incense wafted the confines of Kuriname's living quarters, which served also as his office. He sat traditionally on the floor, mostly in darkness except for three candles. His mind was whirling; too many options, too many obligations, too many thoughts. He knew he was not in "balance."

The ringing of the phone on his desk brought Kuriname's sense of time back to the present. Rising, he stepped to the phone, picking it up on the fifth ring. "Kuriname," he finally said.

"Excuse me Sir; do you have a couple of minutes?"

"Sure Ben," Kuriname answered, recognizing Benjamin Nehen's voice. "Give me a couple of minutes. What do you have?"

"A couple of the men have a question," Nehen said. "Is it alright if we come up?"

"Sure."

Five minutes later, knuckles rapped on the door. "Come," he said. The door opened and three members of his newly created team walked in. The largest of the three, Benjamin Nehen, was dark skinned with high cheek bones and jet black hair cut in a short buzz.

"We have a question, Sir. What are we calling this new team?"

Kuriname motioned for them to find seats. "As a matter of fact, at the moment, we don't have a designation. Why, do you gentlemen have an idea?"

The second man spoke up, Darrell Avonaco; his appearance was similar to Nehen's but he was shorter and stockier. "We do, Sir. Several of us with Native American ancestry have been talking about it."

"If we aren't already labeled," Charles Whitehorse said, "we have a thought."

"Okay, shoot."

Nehen started, "Sir, Darrel and my roots go back to the plains Indians, specifically the Cheyenne. The Cheyenne had six military societies; one was called The Dog Soldiers or Dog Men. The Dog Soldiers stood as a last ditch rear guard group to protect the tribe if attacked. They wore a particular sash, called the Dog Soldier leash. In time of battle, a Dog Soldier would impale the sash to the ground and stand the ground to the death."

"Once committed, they would be either victorious or dead for they had made their stand. They were fierce warriors. Here is a painting from the twentieth century a gentleman named Vic Roseberry created depicting one of them. Would you consider naming the unit The Dog Soldiers?"

"You know," Kuriname said, "I'm vaguely familiar with them. Actually, that's not a bad idea." He pulled out a large piece of drawing paper and placed the Dog Man painting in front of him. With a pencil in hand, he began sketching. "I've been toying with another concept that would honor my Japanese heritage. During the Second World War there was an American combat unit called the 442nd Regimental Combat Team, composed almost entirely of American soldiers of Japanese descent. Even though many of their families were locked away in internment camps, they fought valiantly against the Axis powers; primarily in Europe."

"The 442nd was a self-sufficient force," Kuriname continued. "The 442nd is considered to be the most decorated infantry regiment in the history of the U.S. Army. So many were wounded, its nickname was 'The Purple Heart Battalion.' Their motto was, 'Go for Broke.'" He finished the sketch and surveyed his work. Holding it up he said, "This is a rough, quick idea but what do you think of this as a unit patch?"

442nd Combat Team - Dog Soldiers

Go for Broke

Chapter Forty-Four

Paul Rubenstein sat in the living room, his curiosity pinging around the room; finally he dialed the number on the card.

"Guten Morgen."

"This is Paul Rubenstein; you asked that I call you?"

"Herr Rubenstein, it is nice to hear your voice. Do you know who I am?"

Paul frowned, "I know what the card said but that can't be possible. That person is dead."

"No," the voice said with a gentle laugh. "I assure you my friend that I am very much alive. Is it possible that we speak in person?"

Paul pondered the request for several minutes before his curiosity won out. "It is. Where are you located?"

"Actually, I'm in Honolulu staying at the Astoria Hotel. Can you meet me here?"

"No," Paul answered. "Actually I'm recovering from a slight 'accident.' How about you come here?" Paul gave the address and directions to his home.

Could it be true that he still lives? The voice sounds right, but that is impossible. If it is true what does he want? What could it possibly be about? I thought he was dead. His thoughts had been rolling in his head since the call that morning, now it was afternoon and those thoughts were interrupted by the doorbell ringing. Rubenstein pushed his wire framed glasses back up on his nose and rolled his wheelchair to open the front door.

"Ach du lieber Himmel! Excuse me Herr Rubenstein, Dear God! What has happened to you?" Otto Croenberg, former President of the German Republic, a man whose death had been reported on every major news agency in the world, stood before him.

"I could ask the same thing Mr. President or are you back to being called SS Gruppenführer? What has happened to you? I take it the reports of your death were premature? Come on in."

"Yes and there aren't going to be any more titles that I can see in my future." Otto Croenberg nodded and entered. "Premature but I assure you, absolutely necessary or they would have been accurate. A situation I could not allow. But tell me about you," he said as Paul turned the chair around and began pushing it into the living room.

"Nothing serious," Paul said. "However, it hurts worse than it looks." He said smiling. "Doctor says everything will heal, but I'll be down for the next few weeks. Then a couple of weeks of rehab and everything should be fine. Now Otto, while I was pleased to hear from you, especially since I thought you were dead... How can I be of service?"

"Paul," Croenberg said running one hand over his bald pate. "I appreciate you returning my call; I was not sure that you would. Things in the German Republic have deteriorated, significantly. I fear there is now an unstoppable return to my country's less tolerant history."

"You guys hating Jews again?" Paul asked.

Croenberg smiled to see the bantering between him and Paul still present. "You know that there is no proof of racial superiority by any race, there are no differences between whites, Jews, blacks or Chinese, in any basic sense." Croenberg continued, "But race has always been a convenient excuse, has it not? Going along with Nazi beliefs was simply my way of achieving my goal of power. However, there are new elements of progressivism present in my country that I fear can push everything backwards into history. So much so that I made the decision it was time for me to leave and look for... greener pastures shall we say."

"Progressives, you guys are dealing with them also?"

"They have taken our nationalism, which I did support and turned it into something I can no longer support. You can't deal with them, you can't reason with them. You can't negotiate with Progressives. It is like playing chess with a pigeon. The pigeon knocks over all the pieces, then it shits on the board and then struts around like it won the game."

"So why are you contacting me?" Paul asked.

"I have always held you and Dr. Rourke in high esteem, even though we have had our differences and difficulties."

"You could say that," Paul agreed. "When we first met at Eden City I personally would have enjoyed killing you. But through that whole mess and..." Paul hesitated.

"The difficulties with Zimmer and John Rourke's deceased son, Martin?"

"Exactly," Paul finished. "I have to admit though; I grew to respect your more pragmatic side."

"I told you then that Zimmer was quite insane even if he was a genius. His wish to be master of the earth was the prime example of his insanity; his pathological side. I never hoped to be master of the earth; I was happy to be master of only a part of it. I told you then, I wanted to always have an enemy to oppose him. One force conceiving itself to be 'good' and the other as 'evil.' I however, did not realize the depths the Progressive Movement was willing to sink to."

"We have a similar problem here," Paul said. "The Progressives think they are on cloud nine."

"Just out of curiosity," Croenberg asked. "Where the hell is this cloud nine and where did that dumb expression come from?"

Paul laughed, "I can actually answer that, I did a story about it once. It was tied to an old 1950s radio show called *Johnny Dollar*. Dollar was a high priced insurance investigator who solved cases; he met beautiful women and padded his expense account. Dollar was called on to travel to some distant locale, usually within the United States but sometimes abroad, where he was almost always threatened with personal danger in the course of his investigations."

"Every time Dollar was knocked unconscious he was transported to cloud nine, a wonderful place where a person was blissfully happy. So, if you were on cloud nine you were at the very peak of existence."

"Americans," Croenberg smirked. "Your expressions crack me up; to a foreigner they have no meaning. You take fantasy and spread it across the world to the point that it has lost its original meaning, even for you."

"Alright Otto, cut to the chase. Why are you here?"

Croenberg cleared his throat, suddenly serious. "Paul, I believe there is a substantial threat that could lead to at least an involvement with your government, possibly even its downfall."

Paul said, "You know I'm going to have to alert our authorities?"

Croenberg nodded, "I knew you would want to do that, but I'm going to ask that you do it very surreptitiously. I do not wish the world to know that I am still alive, not yet. Also, I think a 'ghost' may be able to do more help than harm. My preference is we speak to Dr. Rourke confidentially first before involving any recognized agency, is that acceptable to you?"

"I think that will work," Paul said. "Okay if I call him now?"

Chapter Forty-Five

An hour later, John Rourke pulled into Paul's driveway followed by his son Michael's vehicle. Michael got out and turned to his driver, "Stand by Bill, this shouldn't take long." The driver nodded and Michael greeted his father and they walked up and rang the doorbell. "What is the mystery, Paul?" Rourke asked as Paul opened the door and moved out of the way.

"You're not going to believe this, guys. John, I have someone who needs to speak to you."

Michael and John followed Paul into the living room; the figure of a man was outlined by the French doors as he stood looking out into the backyard. He turned; Rourke stopped dead in his tracks. "You have got to be kidding me. You're supposed to be dead."

"Guten Morgen, Herr Mr. President. Please forgive the theatrics, they were unfortunately necessary. Hello Michael." Croenberg crossed the room and extended his hand. "Dr. Rourke, as always it is a pleasure to see you."

Paul gave the Rourkes a quick explanation of how Croenberg had contacted him and the preface for this meeting. Croenberg cleared his throat and pulled an envelope with three closely typed pages from his coat pocket and handed it to John to open. "Several months ago our Bundesamt für Verfassungsschutz, the agency in charge of domestic violence, sent me a report on a gentleman by the name of Peter Vale. Have you ever heard of him?" Michael and Paul both thought for a moment before shaking their heads.

"Indications are Vale was named after his grandfather several generations removed. It was he who created the Milice française or the French Militia. That man, Pierre Laval, was the French Prime Minister, during World War II. Pierre is a masculine given name; it is the French form of the name Peter. Pierre, therefore Peter, originally meant 'rock' or 'stone' in French; Laval means valley. A Vale is a small valley, hence the history of his name."

"If I am not mistaken," John said, "the Milice française, or more simply the Milice, was a paramilitary force created by the Vichy Regime, with German aid, to help fight the French Resistance. It participated in summary executions and assassinations and helped round up Jews and résistants in France for deportation. It was the successor to Joseph Darnand's Service d'ordre légionnaireor the SOL militia."

Croenberg nodded, "Correct, this was their emblem," he said and pointed at the second page of the report spread on the coffee table between them.

"The Milice frequently resorted to torture to extract information or confessions from those whom they rounded up. The French Resistance often considered the Milice to be more dangerous than the German Gestapo and SS because they were Frenchmen who spoke the language fluently, had extensive knowledge of the towns and countryside, and knew people and informers. Vale has created a new organization and I believe he is offering an opportunity to your own Progressive Party."

"Our Bfv had become very concerned about his activities. I referred the report to our Federal Intelligence Service, the Bundesnachrichtendienst, they deal with foreign intelligence. The BDN tracked his movements and they found he had been traveling back and forth to Hawaii under a trade visa."

"What kind of opportunity?" Paul asked.

"That my friend is something I don't know yet. But if I am correct, the end result would be the downfall of Michael Rourke's presidency and a new era for your so-called 'western democracy.'"

Rourke frowned, "But you have no idea what the plan is or the direction he's going in?"

"Not yet," Croenberg said. "All I can tell you is that it appears he has been in clandestine meetings with select members of your Progressive Party; the one we identified specifically was Phillip Greene. Now with my... situation, I fear all I can do is warn you of the threat. I must ask you to keep my identity a secret. The situation in my own country grew to such a level of threat that I had no choice except to remove the target by faking my own demise. I believe I can be of more assistance to you if news of my continued existence is kept quiet."

Michael said, "Otto, I assume you have a cover identity established?"

Croenberg nodded, "I have known for some time that there was a strong potential I would have to disappear, so to speak. I was able to create several secure alter identities that I don't believe can be penetrated or unwoven."

"Then I believe it is time to define what Vale is up to and how the Progressives are involved," Michael said after a nod from John.

"I trust your judgment Michael. I caution we must tread softly; Vale is a very smart but a very bad man."

Chapter Forty-Six

"Mr. President," Tim Shaw said. "I have to tell you that the last week has been disturbing, especially with the veil of secrecy we have had to employ. Even a spy novelist would have had a hard time trying to invent a more complicated or improbable scenario for espionage. Vale has established himself as an 'asset' of staggering potential. He is a professional spymaster and controller of a vast underground network. Vale apparently has the negotiating skills of a master scam artist. By the time the Bfv raided his headquarters in Berlin, all they found were empty file cabinets and litter."

"Croenberg's contact says he wants to place his entire apparatus, 'unpurged and without interruption,' at the service of the American Progressive Party," Michael said.

Shaw nodded, "That appears to be true, and while I don't think Phillip Greene would have invited such a man to his club, he did the next best thing. We think he was able to funnel more than $200 million in party funds to Vale's organization. Directing operations from a clandestine nerve center, Vale has activated his network inside the U.S.A. and kept it connected to his worldwide activities."

Chapter Forty-Seven

Otto Croenberg, in the persona of Darrel Johnson, prepared to go on his "fishing" expedition. His baldness was hidden under a dark, human hair wig; his normal slight German accent was now a practiced mid-western pattern of speech. He was, after all, a master of disguises. His Italian silk suit subtlety proclaimed "money" without being ostentatious. As he previewed his appearance in the lighted makeup mirror, he smiled. His eyebrows were darker and the pencil thin mustache applied perfectly. The carefully prepared pancake makeup had taken several years off his appearance. Now appearing in his mid-forties, he felt ready.

He picked up the ebony walking stick; its polished sterling knob gleamed. He gave a slight tug and right hand twist to the knob and deployed the five and a half-inch, doubled-edged high carbon dagger blade through the rubber tip. Turning the knob several turns to the left, he cocked and relocked the blade, making it undetectable.

Buckling on the metal and polymer sleeve holster rig, and shrugging on the suit coat, he squeezed his right elbow to his side, activating a pressure switch. The stainless Seecamp .32 automatic with black nylon and glass fiber reinforced grips, slid silently and instantly into his hand. He picked one round from the desktop and dropped it into the chamber, then slid and locked the loaded magazine into the bottom of the grip.

This Seecamp had been hidden away in a safe deposit box that had remained sealed since before the Night of the War. It had been a gift from an old friend many years before. Completely restored, it was as functional and trustworthy as the day it came off of the Seecamp production line, so long ago.

Croenberg favored the new 60 grain round made by Lancer Arms, modeled after the old Winchester Super-X Silvertip round. It was considered the most dependable and performance-proven handgun cartridges ever created. Originally developed for law enforcement, the slug boasted a specially engineered jacketed bullet with a muzzle velocity of 970 feet per second and muzzle energy of 125 foot pounds.

Specifically designed for "close up work," the Seecamp wasn't a weapon you would practice fifty or even twenty-five yard shots. Often this genre of weapons was called "mouse" guns because of their small size. Most were notorious for a "stovepipe" malfunction but the Seecamp was as close to perfection as a weapon to be made. If the weapon was cleaned properly, it virtually eliminated the risk of a final round stovepipe jam because of a badly fouled chamber. The other "cure" was to only load six in the magazine, but Croenberg had always said, "I'd rather take a certain six and an almost certain seventh over a certain six and no possibility of a seventh."

Many felt that ball ammunition provided better penetration and hollow points weren't consistent for expansion. While it was true that they had excellent penetration, the streamlined configuration of ball created the smallest temporary wound cavity. Croenberg wanted to ensure a devastating wound cavity; his life depended on it. Hollow points were known to expand better in bare ballistic gelatin than ball. They did not expand as well in heavily clothed gelatin. For that reason, Croenberg usually delivered a shot either to the heart or the skull. After all, at a range of three to five feet, what difference did it make?

The appointment with Phillip Greene was set for 10:00 a.m.

Chapter Forty-Eight

"Come in Mr. Johnson, how may I be of assistance?" Greene asked.

"I believe it is I who may be of assistance to you sir," Croenberg/Johnson said with a smile. "However, before we converse any further, there must be one condition."

Greene sat down behind the desk and dabbed the corner of his mouth with a napkin. Saliva still occasionally dripped as a result of his last encounter with Michael Rourke. "Well, I'm not sure I can agree to anything beforehand. What is your condition?"

"Mr. Greene, I believe that you have recently met with..." He stopped for effect. "Shall we say we have a mutual acquaintance who insists on anonymity? Would you agree that is the case?"

"You mean..." Greene stopped when Johnson raised his right hand.

"As I said, Mr. Greene... anonymity, remember?"

"Ah, yes I see," Greene said thinking of Vale and taking the bait.

"This 'operation' is a delicate matter, would you agree?"

Greene nodded, "Yes that was explained to me by our acquaintance. So why are you here?"

"To explain certain things to you. Our 'principals' were somewhat taken back when we found he had contacted you. They are very uncomfortable about that. They wished me to explain some things to you. First of all, his decision to contact you was against our... protocol. That brings his judgment into question. However, your reputation and positioning have been determined to have some particular and unique value to our principals."

Greene cleared his throat, "I assure you sir, I am the soul of discretion."

"Excellent, I hope so. You see Mr. Greene, you are being evaluated for an increase... both in stature and participation. You have the potential for some excellent returns on your investment... of actions, compliance and loyalty. Loyalty to our principals, not to our acquaintance. Am I making myself clear?"

"Uh, frankly, I'm not sure."

"Our acquaintance has recently made some... questionable decisions. I need you to provide the contents of any further conversations directly to me. You see his continued participation in this venture is being evaluated also."

Greene swallowed the hook, "I believe you are saying that if the evaluation goes badly for him..."

"Exactly, Mr. Greene. You are in a position of becoming his replacement. When he makes contact with you call me at this number." Johnson handed him a card. "You are to keep this meeting confidential, and remember Mr. Greene, you are under surveillance also. If this meeting, if this conversation is shared with anyone, particularly our acquaintance... well, the consequences will be unfortunate."

"Certainly, Mr. Johnson. I understand and please thank your principals for their trust. Again, I assure you, I am the soul of discretion." Croenberg smiled and thought, *Sure you are Mr. Greene.* Greene opened up, listing his involvement and the activities he and Vale had agreed on. After twenty minutes, Croenberg stood and thanked Greene. After the perfunctory handshake, Croenberg left.

Greene sat back down at the desk and wondered at his good fortune. Vale had seemed so in control, so powerful. *Hmmm,* Greene thought then smiled. *Mr. Vale, you may be on your way out and it looks like I could be on my way up.*

* * * * *

Croenberg adjusted his seat belt, turned the ignition key then dialed his phone. "Yes, the meeting went well. Greene is such an idiot, a complete incompetent with an ego the size of the Black Sea. The only thing I believe larger is his innate greed. He is truly a 'Giftzwerg,' an evil little bastard. In any event, we have our mole." Croenberg listened for a moment, checked the chronometer on his dashboard and said, "Okay, I'll be there in thirty minutes." He broke the connection and merged into traffic.

Chapter Forty-Nine

Croenberg pulled the low-slung silver sports car slowly into the parking lot, looking for anything out of the ordinary. Seeing only one other vehicle parked next to the darkened side of a single building, he angled toward it. Stepping out of his car, Croenberg took one last look around the parking lot and walked toward the edge of the building and stood. Suddenly, there was a click behind him in the dark. With a slight nudge of his right elbow, the small .32 auto slid silently down the track of the sleeve mechanism into his hand.

In the darkness, a small flame illuminated the face of John Thomas Rourke as he puffed a thin black cigar to life in the flame from his battered Zippo lighter; there was a slight clunk as he closed the top, extinguishing the flame. "Evening, Herr Croenberg. Thanks for coming."

Croenberg smiled, reset the .32 in its normal position and walked to Rourke. With a slight click of his heels and a quick bow of his head he extended his right hand, "Good evening Generaloberst Dr. Rourke. I trust you are well."

Rourke hesitated and smiled. "Otto, does that little contraption of yours ever deploy on its own and go off accidentally?"

Croenberg looked at his right arm and smiled, "No John," he said with a chuckle. "It has not, I assure you."

Rourke smiled and took the outstretched hand, "Good, now what do you have to report on the meeting with Greene?"

Croenberg smiled, "As I told you, he is an idiot, a complete incompetent with an incredible ego. The good news is you were correct about his innate greed. He does, however, seem pliable enough for our desires and will make an excellent mole. I had determined that... for all of his faults, which will play to our benefit, he will be an excellent source of information for us."

Rourke inhaled deeply and exhaled a wreath of cigar smoke into the night air. "Anything we can use right now?"

Croenberg nodded slightly, "Yes, I believe so. However, Mr. Greene was somewhat guarded and I'm not sure of exactly what to make of it." Croenberg then pulled a small micro recorder from his breast pocket and keyed the play button and nudged the fast forward function. Phillip Greene's voice was somewhat muffled but clearly audible.

Chapter Fifty

John Rourke settled into the driver's seat of his pickup, snapped the seat belt and drove slowly out of the parking lot. Unconsciously, he kept checking his side and rear view mirrors, watching for a tail. Turning left, he merged into traffic and kept pace with the other vehicles. Several random turns later, he relaxed, sure no one was following him.

Four miles from home, the road paralleled the ocean front. The moon peaked out behind the gathering clouds for moments at a time before being hidden again by approaching clouds, heralding an approaching weather front. *Looks like rain,* he thought. He absently pulled out one of his thin cigars and the old Zippo lighter. He rolled the striker wheel and after a couple of puffs had the cigar going. Rounding the curve, he noticed an older car had pulled to the side of the road; someone, a woman, was standing next to it waving a small flashlight with her left hand and supporting herself with her right hand behind her back.

She must have broken down; he thought as he slowed, pulled to the shoulder, and stopped. He slid the cigar into the dashboard ashtray. In his headlights he could see she was probably in her early thirties, long blonde hair braided into a single strand that hung over her right shoulder, almost to her waist. And she was a "looker." He stepped from the cab and began walking the thirty odd feet to her asking, "Car trouble?"

"Yes," she said. "Thanks for stopping, trouble always comes when you least expect it, doesn't it?"

Closing the distance to about twelve feet, Rourke smiled, "Yes that is usually the way it happens. Do you need a lift?"

Smiling provocatively she said, "No Dr. Rourke; what I need is for you to stop right there and raise your hands." A menacing submachine pistol whipped suddenly from behind her back.

Damn it, an ambush, Rourke thought as a man stood up from behind her car. A blinding light jumped from the business end of what Rourke suspected was a tricked out shotgun. Rourke noticed the man's left hand was on the trigger and his right on the slide action. The tactical flashlight held him locked in its glare.

"She said raise your hands," the man said without racking the pump action. Rourke surmised there was already a shell in the chamber. He slowly brought both hands over his head.

"What now?" Rourke asked as his mind flashed through his potential options, finding none.

The blonde moved to Rourke's left as the man rounded the rear of her car and approached him from the right; they were pros enough not to lock the other in a potential cross fire. "Go ahead, get his weapons," the man said gruffly and don't forget that damn Sting knife he carries.

She walked closer to Rourke, stopping just out of his reach and said, "Believe me, I'd prefer not to have to shoot you. That being said, also believe I have no compunction in pulling the trigger if you do not comply."

"Looks like you have the advantage on me, Miss," Rourke said without a smile.

Holding the machine pistol firmly in her right hand, she reached with her left and unzipped Rourke's brown leather bomber jacket. Reaching under his right arm she grasped the CombatMaster and with a slight jerk opened the Alessi trigger guard retention snap and slid the .45 out. She stepped back and shoved the gun into her wide leather belt. Again, smiling sweetly she said, "Now, your knife. I believe you like to carry it on your right hip." She felt along the beltline, found the Sting 1A and jerked it and its sheath out. Stepping back, she secured it also in her belt. "Now, the .45 under your left arm."

As she reached forward, for a scant instant Rourke had an equally scant chance. He moved. With his right hand, he grabbed her left and spun her hard, whipping her in a circle. Almost as if they were dancing, he pulled her in front of his own body and pivoted both of them toward the man with the shotgun. Rourke's left hand went behind his back and snatched the Fighting Bowie from its horizontal sheath in a reverse grip as the shotgunner scrambled quickly toward them, trying to get a clear shot.

Rourke threw the woman forward into his male opponent, hoping if the man shot, the bulk of the projectiles would get her. Stepping forward to follow her body, Rourke slashed upward with the long, sharpened, serrated clip point. He was almost too far off, a half-inch more and he would have missed the man all together. A quarter-inch of the blade sliced through the man's right knuckles; the impact of the woman's body further sweeping the deadly bore of the shotgun further out of alignment with Rourke's head.

Reversing his slash in mid-motion, Rourke drove the six-inch blade into the left side of the man's throat slightly above the juncture of his neck and shoulder. The shotgun fired, but missed. Rourke grabbed the woman's shoulder for stability as he pivoted at the waist; he threw his upper body backward and upward. He sliced the Fighting Bowie, ripping up and out, shredding the man's trachea and all of the major arteries on both sides. The wound was massive, almost decapitating him. The man dropped the shotgun and grabbed at his throat trying to stem the fountains of gore and blood that vomited out of the wound with each beat of his heart.

Rourke racked the primary edge of the Bowie's blade across the back of his other attacker's right hand. It was a sloppy cut, not a clean technique at all, but he didn't have a good angle of attack. She screamed and gunfire erupted from the short barrel of the machine pistol and ended almost as quickly. The severed tendons and ligaments in her hand were no longer able to grasp the weapon's grip. Rourke spun her around to face him and with an upper cut from the skull crusher pummel of his Fighting Bowie; he knocked her out. He wiped off the blade on her skirt as she slid to the ground. Shoving the Bowie back into its horizontal sheath in the small of his back, Rourke jerked his other CombatMaster into play.

He kicked the machine pistol across the road and spun, searching for another threat. Seeing no other attackers, he knelt by the man. Flat on his back, his attacker's neck continued to pump out his life blood with ever decreasing force and volume. With a studied eye, Rourke knew nothing could be done to save the man's life. "You're dying..."

The man looked into Rourke's eyes with a combination of hate and fear, growing weaker with each instant. The only sound he made was a sickening gurgle that created a bloody froth that bubbled from the wound in his throat. The heels of his boot tapped the hard pavement in involuntary spasms. With the muscles in his throat ripped as they were, he just blinked his understanding; a few seconds later, he closed his eyes forever. A few seconds passed before the twitching of his feet stopped and it was quiet again.

Rourke stood and turned to the woman; kneeling down, he first retrieved the .45 she had taken from him and reholstered it. He rolled her over and jerked the Sting and its sheath from her belt, and then he looked at her wounded hand. Pulling the heavy leather belt from around her waist, he fashioned a crude constriction band around her forearm. Satisfied to see the flow of blood slow and then very nearly stop, he picked her up quickly in his arms and walked back to his vehicle.

Opening the passenger door, he slid her into the seat and buckled the seat belt tightly to hold her upright. Rourke rolled down the passenger door window slightly and threaded the end of the belt into it then rolled the window back up. Keeping the arm elevated would further reduce the blood flow. Opening the glove box, Rourke pulled out a rolled up bundle of military 550 paracord.

Taking her uninjured hand, he wrapped several turns around her wrist and tied the hand across her body to the arm rest on that door. Immobilized in this manner, he was satisfied that if she did awaken, she couldn't open the seat belt, untie her hands or open the door and jump out. He pushed the lock and slammed the door shut. He pulled the stainless Detonics .45 from his right shoulder holster and walked to the other side of the truck, climbed into the cab and turned the ignition key.

Taking a quick glance around, he pulled back onto the highway. Pulling the cigar from the ashtray, he relit it and thought, *What the hell was that all about and is there another team ahead of me?* Watching for lights both behind and in front of him, Rourke reversed direction back toward town. He passed two closed gas stations before he found what he needed. At the third he saw it; probably one of the last pay telephone booths on the island. Parking next to it, he climbed out, jerked the handset to his ear and began thumbing several quarters into the machine's pay slot. Tim Shaw answered sleepily, "Yeah, this is Shaw."

Chapter Fifty-One

"Tim, John Rourke. I need you to alert the family, I was ambushed on the way home. My usual route about four miles from home. I need you to get to Emma and the kids as soon as possible and make sure they are alright. I was afraid to go there for fear of someone lying in wait to ambush me there if the first attack failed. Contact the Highway Patrol and have them secure the ambush site. I have a prisoner and I'm headed to the emergency clinic close to home, you know the one. She's hurt but will live; hopefully, we can get some answers. Have one of your units... no, better make that two units, meet me there. It is possible there is a cleanup team waiting on me at any of the hospitals, but I can't see them being able to cover all of the hospitals and the emergency clinics."

Shaw acknowledged and broke the connection. Rourke jogged back to the truck. He looked at her, even unconscious with a big bruise surfacing on her chin she, was lovely in a rather exotic way. She was starting to stir, on her way back to consciousness. *You are a little Barbie Doll, aren't you? But I don't need you to be a problem right now little lady,* he thought and with a modicum of regret, Rourke snapped a right jab to the point of her chin putting her back to sleep.

Three miles later, Rourke pulled into the parking lot of the emergency clinic. As he was removing the blonde's restraints; two cars carrying Tim Shaw's men arrived with red and blue lights flashing. They skidded to a stop; four men from the first car jumped out and moved to set up a security over watch around Rourke. Four from the second vehicle rushed over to Rourke's side. Rourke recognized the senior agent but couldn't recall his name, "We'll take it from here, Mr. Rourke. Are you armed?"

"Yeah," Rourke said. "If two of you can get her inside I have to get to my family and make sure they're alright."

"Like I said, we have it here," the agent said, turning to address one of his men. "Jenkins, take Mr. Rourke to his home... watch your asses. Mr. Rourke, please stay with Agent Jenkins. Phillips..." The agent called over a man from the over watch. "You go with Jenkins and Mr. Rourke as back up." Turning back to Rourke he said, "SSAC Shaw should be there already. We'll secure the scene and the prisoner here. HPD has already been sent to the ambush site to secure it. Go, Mr. Rourke, go!"

Rourke nodded and ran to the sedan where Agent Jenkins already had the engine started. Rourke jumped into the right passenger seat as Agent Phillips jumped in the rear seat behind Jenkins. Before either had their seat belts snapped, Jenkins was out of the parking lot and running Code 3 toward Rourke's home. The unit's radio cracked from under the dash, it was Tim Shaw. He told Rourke he was on the scene with Emma and the kids. "They're fine John—looks like the attack was focused on you. I have alerted the President and the First Family; Paul and Annie are safe also and I have agents with them."

"Thanks Tim. That's great to hear, I'll be there..." He shot a glance to Jenkins. "Traveling at this speed..." Jenkins, with his eyes focused on the road, held up his right hand, fingers splayed. "I'll be there in five minutes," Rourke finished. As he replaced the corded microphone, he said, "Step on it Agent Jenkins."

Jenkins stayed focused, "I've got my foot all the way to the carburetor Mr. Rourke. You just hang on."

Chapter Fifty-Two

Jenkins dry slid the sedan into the driveway; Rourke was out of the car before it fully stopped. He charged past the agent on the front porch and through the front door, "Emma!" he shouted.

"In here, John," she answered from the kitchen.

Rourke turned the corner and saw she was making another pot of coffee; the kids, still half asleep, were sitting at the dining room table. Emma's father, Tim Shaw, sat on a bar stool. Rourke grabbed Emma in a hug, "I'm so glad..." He didn't finish the statement.

Emma hugged him hard, "Are you sure you're okay?" She asked.

Rourke nodded and went to the kids, "You guys okay?"

"Dad, what is going on?" Timothy asked sleepily.

"I'm not sure yet," he said then turned to Shaw. "Thanks," was all Rourke could think of to say.

"No need for thanks John. Look, here's what we know right now. The Highway Patrol recovered the body of an as yet unidentified white male at the ambush site. What the hell did you use on him, a chain saw?"

"No," Rourke said, pulling out the Fighting Bowie. "This; they knew about my Detonics and the Sting 1A but not about the Bowie." Rourke went to the sink and ran water across the blade and handle to remove the blood that had not come off on the blonde girl's skirt. Satisfied, he ran water over his hands to wash away the residue that remained. He picked up a dish towel to dry the knife and his hands but Emma hollered, "No you don't Mr. Rourke!" She handed him several paper towels, "Use these please and throw them away." Rourke complied.

"I couldn't find any identification on the woman either," Rourke said as he disposed of the paper towels in the kitchen garbage container.

"Any clues what this is all about?" Shaw asked.

Rourke shook his head, "Not a one. They didn't give me any time for conversation; when I dropped her off she was still unconscious. It was definitely a snatch job. She called me by name and she knew almost everything about my personal weapons. Any word from the clinic on her condition?"

"They moved her to a military hospital and she's in surgery," Shaw said. "They called in an orthopedic surgeon; his initial exam determined they will be able to save the hand, but he's not sure how much use of it she'll have." Glancing at his wrist watch he continued, "Doc said the surgery should take about two hours. We can talk to her in the morning, but not until."

"I want a 24-hour guard on her," Rourke said.

"Already in place," Shaw nodded. "Looks like she is our only source of information."

Rourke poured sour mash whiskey into a shot glass and slammed it down his throat. "Rest of the family is secure?" Shaw nodded. The adrenal rush was starting to leave Rourke's body as the sour mash warmed his belly. "Guards on them too?" Shaw nodded.

Emma snuggled close into the crook of Rourke's left arm and squeezed him tightly. John kissed her on the head as he poured another shot with his right hand. "How about one of those for me?" Shaw said.

Rourke smiled, "Sorry, thought you were on duty."

"I am, pour me one anyway." Rourke kissed Emma again and reached around her for another glass. As he finished pouring Shaw's drink he said, "We secure outside?" Shaw nodded again. Rourke hugged Emma and said, "Honey, why don't you guys get back to bed. Nothing more is likely to happen now. Tim, lets step out on the patio..."

Chapter Fifty-Three

The clouds that had been blowing in earlier now hung unmoving in the sky, obscuring the moon and stars completely. Rourke pulled one of the patio chairs back from the table; it slid noisily on the patio stones. He pulled out his last cigar, flicked the Zippo into life and sat down. Shaw pulled a cigarette from his pack and accepted a light from John. "John," he said as he sipped his sour mash. "Are you sure you don't know what this attack was about?"

"Tim, it could be anything... but to answer your direct question... no I don't."

"You ever see either of them before?"

Rourke shook his head, "Don't think so. I might have missed the man, but not the woman—blonde Barbie Doll type with a single braid of hair going all the way to her waist."

Setting down his drink and cigarette, Shaw wiped his face with both hands. "Well, it's not like you haven't had enemies; only good thing is most of them are dead."

John inhaled deeply, let out the smoke slowly and took a sip of the whiskey. "Could be Dodd, could be the progressives... I just don't know. I want the whole family guarded until we find out."

Chapter Fifty-Four

Retired Captain Daniel Thomas Hasher, formerly head of operations at the Hopper Information Services Center, was part of President Michael Rourke's ultra secret Lock Out Team; he was also a member of the Progressive Party. Hasher however, had made it clear to Rourke that he was an American first and a Progressive second. He had told Vice President Darkwater, "We can agree to disagree on policies but I hope you are not questioning my loyalty to this country." Darkwater had assured Hasher he had complete faith in him.

"Dan," Darkwater said during the first Lock Out activation, "If I had any questions about you, you would not be sitting here." That was the beginning of a "delicate situation." The investigation was not going to be allowed to go down the path of partisanship and turn into a witch hunt. Darkwater had stated also, "I believe that decisive action, decisive and immediate actions, are on the horizon. The very fabric of this country's political processes are about to be strained and we have to be careful and professional."

The discussions had taken place before the insertion of Wes Sanderson's team on the Kamchatka Peninsula and subsequent rescue of the First Lady at Göbekli Tepe. The investigation was nearing completion and the results had the potential for, as Darkwater had said, "a major political situation of the gravest order."

Chapter Fifty-Five

Peter Vale sat relaxed in the company of Phillip Greene and Captain Dodd. Dodd asked, "What progress have you been able to make?"

Vale smiled and said, "I am happy to report that on Friday, protesters seized the Chancellery Building; that is the seat of government for the German Republic. Occupying almost 130,000 square feet, it is also the largest government headquarters building in the world. By comparison, the new Chancellery Building is ten times the size of the White House. They also established a siege of several governors' offices in the country's west; needless to say, raising the pressure on the government."

"After meeting with the new German President for several hours late Thursday, one protest leader told the crowds he wanted promises that would ensure the release of dozens of protesters detained after clashes with police, and to stop further detentions. They urged the protesters to maintain a shaky truce following violent street battles in the capital, but were booed by demonstrators eager to resume clashes with police."

"So far, the truce has held, but early Friday, protesters broke into the downtown building of the Ministry of Financial Policy, meeting no resistance. One of the protestors told the media, 'We want what is ours. We are the ones who invested our time, money and energy; we cannot have people sleeping in tents all the time.'"

"After seizing the Chancellery, the demonstrators allowed ministry workers to go to work. Then, in other protests, they seized local governors' offices in several western regions on Thursday. Hundreds of protestors broke into the office of the regional governor shouting 'Revolution!' They forced one local governor to sign a resignation letter but then continued to hold the building, refusing to let the workers in."

"Protesters have also taken control of bank offices in four other western cities as of Thursday, though they suffered a setback in one town about ninety miles southeast of Berlin, where police barricaded the governor's building from inside and prevented them from taking control. Police reinforcements arrived later, dispersing the protesters and arresting several dozen of them. The German President meanwhile called for an emergency session of parliament—which is controlled by his loyalists—next week to discuss the tensions. It wasn't clear if his move Thursday reflected his intention to bow to some of the protesters' demands, or was just an attempt to buy some time and try to ease tensions."

Greene interrupted, "I understand that the German Interior Minister issued a statement late Thursday, guaranteeing that police would not take action against the large protest camp on Independence Square. He also urged police not to react to provocations."

Vale nodded, "You are correct. However, with some... encouragement on our part. Remember the demonstrations began abruptly over an agreement with the Europeans who are in favor of a bailout loan from Russia. The protests have been largely peaceful, but we were able to incite the protestors; they turned violent Sunday after the government pushed through harsh anti-protest laws and stonewalled protesters' demands that called for new elections. It has actually been rather simple to engineer. Mob mentality is much more easily manipulated than individual mentality."

"So far, over 200 people have been fatally shot in the clashes Wednesday; the first deaths since the protest began, fueling fears of further escalation. The opposition has blamed the deaths on authorities, but the German Prime Minister said Thursday that the wounds were not caused by police weapons. The protestors claim that as many as fifty protesters were killed in Wednesday's clashes, though they said they have no evidence because the bodies were removed by authorities."

"I understand," Greene said, "protest leaders have set a Thursday evening deadline for the government to make concessions or face renewed clashes. But then pleaded with the crowds to extend the truce, even though the talks with the government have brought literally no visible progress; and, there was no word about meeting the main protesters' demand for early elections."

"Again, you are correct," Vale said, consulting the report. "Goering just released another statement, this one saying, 'When the currency revaluation did not go public for everyone—only for the privileged few who don't need it—we went to the streets to demand it. We recognize this process has taken a long time; after all it affects all of the countries in the world. It takes time.'"

"However, I received a call from several high ranking people in the banking industry who are very familiar with what is going on. They are saying that several bankers have called in their wealthy depositors to do the currency exchange. First, they called them and told them to buy the old currency and the next day bring it in and they will get rich. Well, they are saying that what the bankers don't know is that many of those folks on the wealthy list are really our people, honest people; and, the only thing the bankers are going to get is a set of handcuffs as they leave the bank, headed to a jail cell somewhere in the US. Sounds like the bankers have bit off more than they can chew."

"My sources say the reports are spot on and that we are doing the right thing. So, they are saying just hang in there and we will be at the banks or dealers to await the exchange that is supposed to be for everyone."

Dodd interrupted. "I believe the founder of the World Economic Council has said, 'It's time to press the reset button on the world. The world is complex, it's fast-moving, it's interconnected, and we want to provide a mirror to the world as it is. It is not a meeting devoted to one set of issues. It's a meeting that addresses the complexity of our world.'"

Vale nodded, "And that announcement is being seen as part of the efforts of the WEC for the upcoming yearly jamboree focused on global political and corporate elite. The WEC has as its goal its signature legislation, an ambition no less lofty than to foster an environment where the myriad problems and challenges facing today's world can be tackled head on. It is time to push the reset button. We have been successful in creating a world still caught up in a crisis-management mode."

"The crisis is coming and frankly, as long as we have control of the process, we will be successful. Now we are beginning to focus on some more conservative, constructive and strategic plans. We are getting ours, so to speak. The danger is we now have to allow some of the 'little people' to get theirs. But in doing so, it has to be carefully handled. This is where it can get complicated and dangerous. There has never been the opportunity at any time in the world's history where so many 'stakeholders' of our global future have had this chance. And they are all united by the mission of improving the state of the world."

"They believe, with some confidence I might add, that it appears the world is coming back into a stable global economy following the difficult post-financial crises years, but it has been like a runner struggling with a heavy load on his shoulders. It is in fact, the element of superstitious reinforcement that is working to our benefit. That irrational belief is that an action, or set of circumstances not logically related to a course of events, can influence an outcome. That is being perpetuated by a belief in a series of practices we have been able to irrationally maintain because they are ignorant of the laws of nature and their own faith in magic or chance."

Greene asked, "So what's next, Mr. Vale?"

Vale smiled, "The next part has two elements. Increased confusion and turmoil followed by our domination of the financial structure for the entire planet. In short gentlemen, we win. With our Chinese and Russian allies, the American Dollar and New Germany's Mark will become devalued overnight. That will mean the German Republic's currency will dominate the world along with the Chinese Yen and the Russian Ruble. We win without ever firing a shot. Captain Dodd, if you don't mind me asking, how is our 'little ally' doing?"

Dodd smiled, "Very nicely Mr. Vale, he and his friends are making their presence known already."

Chapter Fifty-Six

Paul smiled, able to finally walk with a cane. His last x-rays had shown the crack in his femur was healing nicely and he was glad. He had hated his time in the wheelchair even though he knew it was necessary. The doctors had finally released him from the walking boot and crutches, to the walker. "The cane gives me more stability, particularly on uneven terrain," he told Annie. "I think it gives me a rather distinguished, almost dapper appearance." Annie just smiled. Paul knew the necessity of the cane would wane quickly away, but he toyed with the idea of keeping it. He particularly liked that it had a two-foot blade hidden in it.

John Rourke, his son Tim, Paul and his son Jack walked along the beach; these walks had become a habit. In the beginning it had been therapy for Paul's leg but lately had simply been a good time for the guys to get together and chat. Recently, the boys had been focusing on weapons; especially Jack. Today, it was about knives; especially the new Fighting Bowie John was showing them. "John," Paul asked. "I've always wondered why none of the knives you carry have a blood groove?"

"Actually, over the years Paul, I've had several that did."

"Grandpa, what is a blood groove for?" Jack asked. "What does it do?"

"Good questions; there are several answers. In reality, the blood groove or blood curve probably came from a channel on a sword that is called a 'fuller.' A lot of folks believe the blood groove releases a vacuum when the knife is thrust into a person. Others believe it holds no functional use and is purely decorative."

"The first theory states that the blood groove is present to help when pulling a knife out of a person or an animal. It has been said that a person or an animal's muscles will contract around the knife blade, and that this causes a vacuum. That would make the knife difficult to withdraw. But with a blood groove, blood is supposed to run through the blood groove and break the suction, so the knife can be withdrawn with less difficulty."

Tim said, "I can't see how that suction could be real."

John agreed, "I don't think it ever really happens. Frankly, I never noticed a difference in the difficulty of withdrawing a knife with a blood groove versus one without. My thought is if your knife can cut its way in, it can just as easily cut its way out, with or without a blood groove. Now, to the second theory, I am going to change the term from 'blood groove' to a 'fuller.' This one has a grain of truth to it. While a fuller does play a functional role on a short knife, it is really insignificant. I think the fuller plays more of a strictly decorative role on knives or swords under two feet long. It has what I call 'the GDI' factor."

"What's that?" Jack asked.

Rourke laughed, "It stands for Guys Dig It. They look really cool and dangerous, most of the time whatever has the GDI going for it really doesn't have much function; on a smaller knife the blood grove is like that. On a bigger blade however, it stiffens and lightens the blade."

"Does a lighter blade feel stiffer?" Jack asked.

Rourke nodded, "I think it just feels stiffer to the user who is waving it around—because it's stiffer for its weight. Years ago, I read a report by a twentieth century master bladesmith named Jim Hrisoulas; I think he explained well. He said a blood groove potentially could serve two functions. You see, if you are forging a blade with a fuller, that actually widens the blade, so you use less material than you would if you forged an unfullered blade. If you're doing stock removal, the blade would also be lighter, as you would be removing the material instead of leaving it there."

"It does stiffen the blade. He said that in an unfullered blade, you only have a 'single' center spine. This is especially true in terms of the flattened diamond cross section common to most unfullered double-edged blades. This cross section would be rather 'whippy' on a blade that is close to three feet long. Fullering produces two 'spines' on the blade, one on each side of the fuller, where the edge bevels and comes in contact with the fuller. This stiffens the blade; the difference between a non-fullered blade and a fullered one is quite remarkable."

"He also said that when combined with proper tapering, proper heat treating and tempering, a fullered blade will, without a doubt, be anywhere from twenty to thirty-five percent lighter than a non-fullered blade and without any sacrifice of strength or blade integrity."

Chapter Fifty-Seven

The next afternoon, accompanied by Rubenstein, Croenberg entered John Rourke's home with a slight bow and click of his heels. He produced a silken bag with a bottle inside and he said, "I brought a bottle of very old Remy Martin V.S.O.P.—a brandy I have saved for a special occasion. Being here with you two certainly qualifies. Do you have a snifter?"

"No, unfortunately I don't," Rourke said.

Croenberg waved his hand in dismissal, "How about any short-stemmed glassware that has a wide bottom and a relatively narrow top. The large surface area of the contained liquid helps evaporate it; the narrow top traps the aroma inside the glass, while the rounded bottom allows the glass to be cupped in the hand, thus warming the liquor. Most snifters will hold between six to eight ounces, but are almost always filled to only a small part of their capacity," Croenburg said, clearly pleased with his status as a connoisseur.

"I believe so, let me look," Rourke said with a smile and went to the crystal cabinet. "How about these?"

"That will do nicely, John. Paul, would you care to join us?"

"Yes, thank you. Let's step out on the patio," Paul said. "I also brought a gift." He produced three fine cigars and a polished cutter from his pocket. He withdrew a small black box from his other pocket and sat it and the other items on the counter in front of Rourke.

"For me?" Rourke asked.

"Yes, Emma told me your other one has just about given up the ghost," Paul said. "I know you will probably have it restored but maybe this will serve you in the interim, or you might just decide to retire the old one all together."

Rourke took the top of the box off, inside was a Zippo lighter with a street chrome finish. In two lines on the front part of the upper case was engraved, "THE SURVIVALIST." Below is was the JTR brand Paul had seen on the Fighting Bowie knife made by Martin Knives so long ago. John stared at the lighter, and looked at Paul, "Thank you my friend, I really appreciate it."

"Go ahead light up; it's ready to use. Truthfully, that old battered one needs to be retired," Paul said with a smirk. "It is becoming an embarrassment. Now you have a new one that I'm sure in no time will be almost as battered as its predecessor."

As the three walked outside, John Rourke picked up the cutter from the counter and snipped off the tip of one of the cigars. Stepping through the door he flipped the Zippo's top open, rolled the striker wheel, producing a blue yellow flame. Rourke smiled to himself, it was the first time in a long time he had lit a thin dark cigar from an un-battered Zippo lighter.

As they took seats around the patio table, Croenberg asked, "Have either of you ever wondered if a shadowy group of obscenely wealthy elitists control the world? Do men and women with enormous amounts of money really run the world from behind the scenes? The answers are yes there is, and yes they do. Have you ever heard of something called The Cabal?"

John nodded, "Yes, in the twentieth century there was one. I don't know if it was an urban legend or simply part of one of the conspiracy theories that were being floated around. Frankly, I never put much faith in the story or really even understood what it was about."

Croenberg took the proffered cutter from Paul and snipped the end of his cigar. Pulling a wooden strike anywhere match from his pocket, he struck it on the sole of his left shoe then held the tip of the cigar in the flame until it blackened. "I know you have your Zippo, but the best way to light a good cigar is with the flame of wood after all of the sulfur has burned off," he explained.

Taking a deep inhalation, Croenburg nodded his approval to Paul. "Excellent. Now, a Cabal is a simply a group of people united in some close design together, usually to promote their private views or interests, often by intrigue. Cabals most often are rather secret societies composed of a few designing persons, but at other times are manifestations of emergent behavior in a society on the part of a community of persons who have well established public affiliation or kinship. The term can also be used to refer to the designs of such persons or to the practical consequences of their emergent behavior, and also holds a general meaning of intrigue and conspiracy."

Paul lit his cigar and said, "I know the use of the term usually carries strong connotations of shadowy corners, back rooms, and insidious influence."

"Yes," Croenberg said. "The word was first associated with a group of ministers of King Charles, including Sir Thomas Clifford, Lord Arlington, the Duke of Buckingham, Lord Ashley, and Lord Lauderdale; coincidentally their initials spelled CABAL, they were the signatories of the secret Treaty of Dover. It allied England and France in a prospective war against the Netherlands. However, that Cabal never really unified in its members' aims and sympathies, and fell apart by 1672 and ran out of power."

Croenberg lifted the glass of brandy and dipped the cigar tip in the liquor, "Look, most of us tend to think of money as a convenient way to conduct transactions, but the truth is that it also represents power and control. And today we live in a system in which the super-rich pull all the strings. When I am talking about the ultra-wealthy, I am not just talking about people who have a few million dollars. These ultra-wealthy have enough money sitting in banks around the world to buy all of the goods and services produced in the world during the course of an entire year; and, still be able to pay off the entire national debts of every country. That is an amount of money so large that it is almost incomprehensible."

"Under this system, all the rest of us are debt slaves, including our own governments. Just look around—everyone is drowning in debt, and all of that debt is making the ultra-wealthy even wealthier. But the ultra-wealthy don't just sit on all of that wealth; they use some of it to dominate the affairs of the nations. The ultra-wealthy own virtually every major bank and every major corporation on the planet."

"They use a vast network of secret societies, think tanks, and charitable organizations to advance their agendas and to keep their members in line. They control how we view the world through their ownership of the media and their dominance over our educational system.

They fund the campaigns of most of our politicians and they exert a tremendous amount of influence over international organizations such as the United Nations, the International Monetary Fund, and the World Bank."

"When you step back and take a look at the big picture, there is little doubt about who runs the world. It is just that most people don't want to admit the truth. The ultra-wealthy don't run down and put their money in the local bank like you and I do. Instead, they tend to stash their assets in places where they won't be taxed, in offshore accounts. According to a report that was released last summer, the global elite have up to 45 trillion dollars stashed in offshore banks around the globe."

"Your U.S. Gross Domestic Product stands at about 15 trillion dollars, and the U.S. national debt is sitting at about 16 trillion dollars, so you could add them both together and you still wouldn't hit 32 trillion dollars. And of course that does not even count the money that is stashed in other locations that the study did not account for; and, it does not count all of the wealth that the global elite have in hard assets such as real estate, precious metals, art, yachts, etc."

"The global elite have really hoarded an incredible amount of wealth in these troubled times. These individuals and their families have as much as 32 trillion dollars of hidden financial assets in offshore tax havens, representing up to 280 billion in lost income tax revenues. One of my reports estimates the extent of global private financial wealth held in offshore accounts—excluding non-financial assets such as real estate, gold, yachts, and racehorses—at between 21 and 32 trillion dollars. The research was carried out by a young investigator from our own Department of the Treasury; he was a remarkable young man. He compiled his research using data from the World Bank, International Monetary Fund, United Nations, and central banks."

"You said 'was,'" Rourke noted.

Chapter Fifty-Eight

"I did," Croenberg continued, "he was found the victim of an apparent suicide. He supposedly overdosed, but I know that not to be the case. He was a strong amateur athlete and notably against drugs. He even refused offers from me to share this fine brandy. I'll come back to that point."

"In any event," he continued, "as I mentioned previously, the global elite just don't have a lot of money. They also basically own just about every major bank and every major corporation on the entire planet. According to him, more than 40,000 transnational corporations conducted by the Swiss Federal Institute of Technology in Zurich discovered that a very small core group of huge banks, and giant predator corporations, are attempting to dominate the entire global economic system. His analysis of the relationships between several hundred transnational corporations has identified a small group of companies, mainly banks, with disproportionate power over the global economy. He found that this core group consists of just 150 very tightly knit companies."

"When he further untangled the web of ownership, all of the ownership was held by other members of that group and they already control forty percent of the total wealth in the network."

"In effect, less than one percent of the companies were able to gain control of forty percent of the entire world economy. These elite often hide behind layers and layers of ownership, but the truth is that thanks to interlocking corporate relationships, the elite basically control almost every Fortune 500 corporation in the world."

"That amount of power and control, is hard to even contemplate much less describe," Paul said.

Croenberg agreed, "Its roots go back a long way. Back in 1922, a New York City Mayor named John F. Hylan first brought it to light. He said the real menace of our Republic is the invisible government, which 'like a giant octopus sprawls its slimy legs over our cities, states and nation.' He said that at the 'head of this octopus are special interests and a small group of powerful banking houses generally referred to as the international bankers. The little coterie of powerful international bankers virtually runs the United States government for their own selfish purposes.'"

"He saw they were practically controlling both parties, drafting political platforms using the leading men of private organizations, and plunging into high public offices only those candidates amenable to the dictates of corrupt big business."

"Those international bankers and special interests controlled the majority of the newspapers and magazines in this country and, we now know, the world. They used the columns of these papers to club into submission or drive out of office public officials who refused to do the bidding of the powerful corrupt cliques of that invisible government. It operated under cover of a self-created screen and seized the executive officers, legislative bodies, schools, courts, newspapers, and every agency created for the public protection."

"These international bankers created the central banks of the world, including the Federal Reserve, and they used those central banks to get the governments of the world ensnared in endless cycles of debt from which there is no escape. Government debt is, after all, the way to 'legitimately' take money from everyone else, transfer it to the government, and then transfer it into the pockets of the ultra-wealthy."

Rourke shook his head; the data was confusing. "I thought all of that ended the Night of the War. You're saying it didn't?"

"No, the Cabal, like the rest of the world was stunned and crippled. In fact, I don't think many of the original families survived. Of course, that is impossible to verify. The world entered a period of darkness and records simply are not available to examine. I can tell you this, there is a Cabal. I don't know whether it is the remnants of the original one or if someone discovered their hidden resources and activated a new one. But it is a verifiable fact; the Cabal... a Cabal exists."

"For more than a century now, ideological extremists at either end of the political spectrum have seized power that they intend to wield over American political and economic institutions as well as those in all of the other countries. They are in fact part of a secret Cabal characterized as 'internationalists' and of conspiring with others around the world to build a more integrated global political and economic structure — one world, if you will."

"You know, even today, almost all members of Congress absolutely refuse to criticize the Federal Reserve System," Paul said.

Croenberg nodded again, "The last to do so was probably your Congressman Louis T. McFadden who delivered to the U.S. House of Representatives in 1932. He claimed America had one of the most corrupt institutions the world has ever known. His was talking about the Federal Reserve Board and the Federal Reserve Banks. He said the Federal Reserve Board, a Government board, had cheated the Government of the United States and the people of the United States out of enough money to pay the national debt. It had cost the country enough money to pay the national debt several times over. He went on to say, and I'm paraphrasing, 'that evil institution has impoverished and ruined the people of the United States, has bankrupted itself, and has practically bankrupted our Government.'"

"He claimed it had done all of this through the defects of the law under which it operates, through the maladministration of that law by the Federal Reserve Board, and through the corrupt practices of the 'moneyed vultures' who controlled it. While most Americans believed that the Federal Reserve is a 'federal agency,' that wasn't true. The stockholders in the twelve regional Federal Reserve Banks are the privately owned banks that fall under the Federal Reserve System. These banks include all national banks, chartered by the federal government, and those state-chartered banks that wish to join and meet certain requirements.'"

"His point was these ultra-wealthy international bankers have not just done this kind of thing in the United States, but their goal was to create a global financial system that they would dominate and control. These 'financial capitalists' had another far-reaching aim, nothing less than to create a world system of financial control in private hands able to dominate the political system of each country and the economy of the world as a whole. That system was controlled in a feudalist fashion by the central banks of the world acting in concert, by secret agreements arrived at in frequent private meetings and conferences."

143

"Congressman McFadden asked, 'Have you ever wondered why things never seem to change in Washington D.C. no matter who we vote for? Well, it is because both parties are owned by the establishment. It would be nice to think the American people are in control of who runs things in the U.S., but that is not how it works in the real world.' In the real world, the politician that raises more money wins more than eighty percent of the time in national races. Our politicians are not stupid—they are going to be very good to the people who can give them the giant piles of money that they need for their campaigns. And the people who can do that are the ultra-wealthy and the giant corporations that the ultra-wealthy control. Are you starting to get the picture? There is a reason why the ultra-wealthy are referred to as 'the establishment.' They have set up a system that greatly benefits them and allows them to pull the strings."

"I know that no one owns Michael," Rourke said. "But going on your premise, who's running the world? And why haven't we heard about this before?"

Croenberg said, "Silence is a commodity that can be bought and paid for by these people. Those they cannot buy, like my researcher, they kill."

Chapter Fifty-Nine

The next morning, Michael and John Rourke sat alone in the conference room, awaiting the start of yet another meeting. Albeit this one would be different, at least that was their hope. "You have any idea what this dynamic information is supposed to be about?" John asked his son.

"Not really, all I know is that General Sullivan asked for the meeting and specified he thought you ought to be here," Michael answered.

The Marine Guard outside knocked on the door before stepping in, "Sir, they're here."

"Send them in," Michael instructed as he and John stood to greet the new arrivals. General Sullivan followed by Colonel John "Mad Jack" Ball entered.

Sullivan saluted, "Good morning, Mr. President... Mr. Rourke. I appreciate your time. I think you'll find this interesting. You know Colonel Ball?"

Michael shook hands with Ball, "No, but it is my pleasure. I've heard a lot about you from my father."

"Mr. President, it's my honor."

"Morning Jack," John said. "You guys want some coffee?"

"Yes, thank you," Sullivan said.

"I'll get it," Ball said, as he walked to the credenza and poured two cups. "Either of you ready for a refill?"

Michael shook his head but John offered his cup. Sullivan opened his attaché case and powered up his laptop. "Things got so crazy when it became necessary to rescue the First Lady, the original purpose of this mission sort of slid under the carpet. I want to show you what she found. Colonel Ball was sent primarily to search for this information and luckily he found it. You will remember that the First Lady was interested in examining several stone pillars at Göbekli Tepe. It has been supposed this could actually be the site of the temple put up by Noah and his family following the Great Deluge."

"The site includes several massive carved stones about 11,000 years old, crafted and arranged by prehistoric people who had not yet developed metal tools or even pottery. These megaliths predate Stonehenge by some 6,000 years. Currently, we are convinced it's the site of the world's oldest temple."

"It is composed of several ringed structures; each ring has a roughly similar layout. In the center are two large stone T-shaped pillars encircled by slightly smaller stones facing inward. The tallest pillars tower sixteen feet and weigh between seven and ten tons. We think it was the first human-built holy place," he said. "Actually, the first 'cathedral on a hill.'"

"When Göbekli Tepe was first examined, it was dismissed by scholars and anthropologists in the 1960s. Recently, the broken pieces of limestone that earlier surveyors had mistaken for gravestones took on a different meaning. I'm not going into the Biblical or theological connections; I will say that archaeologists have their theories. Evidence perhaps, of the irresistible human urge to explain the unexplainable."

"There is a surprising lack of evidence that people lived right there, which researchers say argues against its use as a settlement or even a place where, for instance, clan leaders gathered. Göbekli Tepe's pillar carvings are dominated not by edible prey like deer and cattle but by menacing creatures such as lions, spiders, snakes, and scorpions. It's a scary, fantastic world of nasty-looking beasts. One theory that seems to have gathered a greater degree of validity is that this is not only a spiritual meeting place but also the world's first library; 6,000 years before a written language was developed."

"Mrs. Rourke found the proof that there is definitely some connection between events playing out today and the history that was from so long ago. Fortunately, she had previsions to secure the information and, equally fortunately, her attackers didn't find it. Look at these," he said, as he activated the view screen.

Images similar to ones Michael and John were familiar with came up. Michael leaned forward and pointed, "Can you enhance that one?"

"Yes, Sir," Sullivan said hitting a flurry of key strokes.

"Dad, is that what I think it is?"

John studied the image, "Can you enlarge this, General?" Sullivan hit two buttons and the image filled the screen. It was a color photo of one the stone pillars. Instead of being covered with images of beasts and birds, it held only two images. The first appeared to be a drawing of a ship remarkably identical to the UFO John had recovered and was now being examined by Colonel Rodney Thorne and flight engineers. The other was a representation of something John had seen on the belt buckle of a dead alien he had examined so long ago in the frozen waste land of Canada above the Arctic Circle. The same emblem that had formed the tattoos he had discovered on the chest of clones.

He looked back at his son. "Yes, Michael this is exactly what you think it is."

Chapter Sixty

Following the Sullivan briefing, John arranged for a conversation with Jose Zima, the linguist from Mid-Wake. Rourke's head was swirling with the implications; and though tired, tried to clear his mind to focus on the conversation at hand.

"Dr. Rourke," Zima said, "I have a story to relate. When the last President of the original United States, Andrew Connelly, had determined to commit suicide rather than be captured, he gave an envelope that contained two letters to the chief of his Secret Service detail, Mike Clemmer. One letter was to the American people; it was published and now is one of our national documents. But Clemmer was never able to deliver the one to the Connelly's wife, Marilyn. Fourteen years ago, the letter to the First Lady surfaced."

Handwritten at the bottom were a series of letters and figures. Everyone thought the president, about to commit suicide, had lost it and scribbled nonsense. The message remained a mystery for years."

"Ten days ago one of our cryptanalysts, who has a passion for puzzle solving, stumbled across it in a magazine article. He recognized it was an obscure code and he set out to decode it. He reasoned that it was probably a book cipher, that is a cipher or code in which the key is some aspect of a book or other piece of text. Books are common and widely available in modern times; however users of book ciphers take the position that the details of the key are sufficiently well hidden from attackers in practice. This is in some ways an example of security by obscurity. It is typically essential that both correspondents not only have the same book, but the same edition."

"Yes," Rourke said, "I'm familiar with them. Book ciphers work by replacing words in the plain text of a message with the location of words from the book being used, realizing the code is to replace individual letters rather than words and those letters are identified by numbers. For example, 2/15/3 would indicate page two, line fifteen, third letter."

Zima nodded. "Exactly, the main strength of a book cipher is the key. The sender and receiver of encoded messages can agree to use any book or other publication available to both of them as the key to their cipher. Someone intercepting the message and attempting to decode it, unless they are a skilled cryptographer, must somehow identify the key from a huge number of possibilities available. Anyway, he found it was not gibberish after all. President Connelly and Mrs. Connelly were both fond of the poet John Greenleaf Whittier. I won't bother you with the details; suffice it to say the key to the code was from the illustrated 1867 hardcover edition of Maud Mueller. It was a romantic poem published in 1854 that dealt with a young woman named Maud who meets the love of her life, but neither of them react to their meeting and both grow old separately. Seems an old friend had given the President two copies and they were the same edition; each had the original cloth covering. My analyst found what is probably the only surviving copy in the Library of Congress and, in less than 20 minutes, had it deciphered."

"And?"

"The President had directed his wife to go to a specific location when things settled down. The location has been determined to be 43 degrees, 52 minutes, 41 seconds North by 103 degrees, 27 minutes, 30 seconds West. Do you know where that is?"

John shook his head, Zima continued. "A forgotten national monument called Mount Rushmore in what used to be South Dakota. It has busts of four former presidents: Washington, Jefferson, Lincoln, and Teddy Roosevelt; each sixty feet tall. Now it sits locked, possibly forever, under probably a couple of hundred feet of glacial ice."

John smiled, "I know Mount Rushmore. I was there several times before the Night of the War. If my memory serves, it took about fourteen years to complete Mount Rushmore and several hundred men and women to carve the monument. Incredibly, no one died while building Mount Rushmore, although some of the workers died later of the lung condition silicosis. They had inhaled dust during the carving of the granite. I thought it had been destroyed."

Zima shook his head, "Nope, still there, but it has faded from general knowledge. Here's the point of why I asked you to meet with me. It seems that

Gutzon Borglum, the monument sculptor, built an interesting special feature that a lot of people knew about initially but was forgotten over the next two decades. He included a 'Hall of Records' in the design, the goal being to create a repository for our nation's charter documents and history. In 1941, when Borglum died, work on the Hall came to a halt. Then, in the mid-1970s, the Hall of Records was completed in secret under military contract; we still don't know the Hall's dimensions. Several items with the story of our nation were sealed in a vault in the unfinished Hall of Records."

"Like what?" Rourke asked. His interest peaked.

"Sixteen porcelain enamel panels containing the text from the Declaration of Independence, the Constitution, and the Bill of Rights, along with a biography of Borglum, and the story of the presidents were sealed in a teakwood box, and then placed in a titanium vault, and finally sealed shut under the weight of a 1,200 pound granite capstone inside the unfinished hall. It seems however, that these were not the only items placed in the Hall of Records."

"Those documents were to remain buried for thousands of years. Borglum literally had it in mind to send the message of our country to future civilizations. He said, 'you might as well drop a letter into the world's postal service without an address or signature, as to send that carved mountain into history without identification.' The public never had access to the Hall of Records because the Hall is located behind the heads, near the cliffs—public safety was a concern. Very few people even knew it existed."

Rourke frowned, "You mentioned some other items were placed in storage, any idea what?"

Zima smiled again, "Yes, in the days and weeks before the Night of the War, tensions were climbing. The situation kept vacillating between imminent war and possible peace. No one knew for sure which way the pendulum would swing. The last president of the original United States realized that while peace was possible, it was improbable. Our studies show that just days before the Night of the War, Connelly ordered the original documents associated with those sixteen panels to be transported from their public locations in Washington and placed for safe keeping in the Hall of Records then had the Hall resealed by a company of combat engineers; all in complete secrecy."

"We also believe a copy of the original report concerning the alien contact with the German government in 1933 that had been smuggled out of pre-war Germany by one of our operatives. An original, never declassified report on the Roswell incident, as well as what are referred to as 'artifacts' from the crash, went to the Hall. We also believe that a copy of the formal agreement between an alien race and the U.S. Government held at Holliman Air Force Base in 1954 was included."

"The terms of this agreement supposedly allowed for an exchange of technology, of anti-gravity, metals, alloys, and environmental technologies to assist the earth with free energy and medical application regarding the human body. In exchange the aliens would be allowed to study the human development, both in the emotional and consciousness makeup, and to reside here on Earth. That particular document, and original exchange material, in fact had been stored in the Blue Moon NSA facility, but was moved to the Hall of Records shortly after the Night of the War to protect them. And the biggest possibility is the President's Book of Secrets, long thought to be an urban legend, is housed there also."

Rourke immediately perked up. "You think it is real after all?"

"Total speculation on the Book," Zima admitted.

"Jose, do you believe these records could still be in this Hall of Records?"

Zima nodded, "We do and we think we have located it after all of these years. Problem is, like I said, it is buried under a lot of ice."

Rourke sat for a long minute deep in thought before asking, "But you think it is possible the Hall of Records still exists and is still sealed?"

"Actually, I think it is probable. We have found no indications that any attempt to retrieve the materials was made after the war. Within those next 100 years, when humanity was trying to survive, the glaciations across North America were completed and the monument faded into history. Plus the fact we are in possession of what we believe is the only remaining document that ever addressed the movement of the materials to the Hall."

"Lastly, is the fact that the letter to President Connelly's wife, Marilyn, wasn't deciphered until ten days ago. And that was more of a pure accident than anything. I think the Hall of Records still lies in the granite around the presidential statues, completely undisturbed."

"Then," Rourke said, "that could be where we'll find the answers we're looking for." Rourke's thoughts were scattered, so much information... so little actual data. "Jose, there is a lot going on and I feel like something my dad said a long time ago."

"What's that?"

Rourke took a deep breath, "He said, 'I feel like I'm trying to shoot a black bird in a dark room at night with a BB gun.' He was talking about trying to make a decision with damn few facts and a lot of speculation. There may, and I underscore may, be only one place to find some historic facts I can use to answer these questions. The problem is we're probably going to need a way to decipher those answers, and that technology no longer exists in this world."

Chapter Sixty-One

Rourke walked slowly out to the parking lot and climbed into his car; he was still weighing the possibilities of Zima's theory. He sat there with his hand on the key without turning the ignition, *Could this be the answer, the proof? It could be an interesting gamble. I agree with Jose,* Rourke thought. *Probably the Hall of Records has remained sealed all of these years and if it has...*

Rourke had heard the conspiracy theory and legend that the Presidents of the United States have passed down a book from George Washington to Andrew Connelly. *I really thought it was a legend,* he reflected, *but it was rumored to have added facts and histories, earth-shattering in scope and implications, and that this book's location is only known to the President and the National Librarian of Congress. If a president died unexpectedly, as with the Lincoln and Kennedy assassinations, the National Librarian would inform the next President of the book. After each President leaves office, the location is changed.*

If it shows the truth about the alien landings at Roswell, New Mexico and Rendlesham Air Base, in the UK, and many other UFO events, that could be invaluable with the threat and conspiracies we have going. Plus I'd like to know the truth about the JFK and RFK assassinations; the location of the Holy Grail—tying in with the Fort Knox conspiracy theory; the fates of various high-ranking Nazis following World War II—and the facts concerning the U. S. government's assistance of them; even the identity of the Antichrist.

Assuming there is a book, and assuming it identifies the Antichrist, we are led to wonder if he and that President are on the same side, or one and the same person. Or if that President feared for Earth's immediate future. Even more insidious, in terms of realism, is the claim that the book told of the Vietnam War before it took place and also told of the imminent attack by Russia, which initiated World War III.

Rourke flipped open a small notebook and started writing. Prior to President Andrew Connelly, only eight American presidents had died while in office—most by natural circumstance such as illness. In 1841, William Henry Harrison first became ill with a cold and thirty days, twelve hours and thirty minutes later, died. The next was Zachary Taylor, his cause of death has never been fully established, but has always been thought to be severe gastroenteritis.

Lincoln was next, his assassination occurring just five days after Robert E. Lee surrendered to Ulysses S. Grant and was followed by James A. Garfield who was shot just four months into his term as America's 20th President. He lingered on throughout the summer but did not survive his injuries. William McKinley was shot by Leon Czogosz on September 6, 1901 and died nine days later. Warren G. Harding's sudden death in 1923 led to theories he had been poisoned or committed suicide. Suicide appeared unlikely since he was planning for a second term election. Some thought an affair with a mistress had led Mrs. Harding to poison her husband but symptoms prior to his death pointed to congestive heart failure.

Franklin D. Roosevelt was the next president to die in office in 1945. His death was attributed to a massive cerebral hemorrhage or stroke. John F. Kennedy was assassinated at 12:30p.m. Central Standard Time on Friday November 22, 1963.

Little was actually known about President Connelly's last hours. His death had not taken as long as his some of his predecessors, nor was it as immediate as Lincoln's and Kennedy's. Zima had said a Rear Admiral Corbin told Connelly, "They—the Russians—got way too much of our stuff while it was on the ground. Sixty percent of the U.S. population was estimated to be dead or dying—about 145 million people."

But the details of almost everything else were lost. The Chief of Connelly's Secret Service detail, Mike Clemmer, later reported that as his last acts as President of the United States, Connelly handed him an envelope with the presidential seal in the upper left corner. Then Connelly said, "And now, give me your revolver. That's an order, Mike. There are two letters in the envelope. One is to my wife; the other is to the American people. Thurston Potter knows what to do with them. This is my last order, Mike. Give me your gun."

Clemmer reported he had wiped his palms on the sides of his trouser legs and reached under his jacket to his right hip. The president watched as he produced a short-barreled, shiny revolver. "I don't know much about guns,

Mike. Always wanted to try them, but never had the time. Does yours have a safety catch?"

Clemmer said, "No, sir. Revolvers don't. Mr. President, you can't. I can't let you."

"You've got to, Mike. If I stay alive, the Russians will find me and use me. If I die, there will be no government left to capitulate, and free Americans will go on fighting until there is a government again—another elected government that will throw the Soviets out. If they get me, it's all over for all of us."

"But Mr. President—they'll never get into Mount Lincoln."

"You know that's not true," the president said. "And if we're totally cut off, they've got a capitulation anyway. But if the American people know I'm gone, then the Soviets... no matter what they do... can't lie to the American people that the United States has surrendered. It's the only way. Now, give me the gun."

The president looked away from Mike Clemmer and extended his right hand, lighting a cigarette with his left. Mike Clemmer placed his revolver in the President's outstretched right hand and walked out of the room.

*****

Not that it mattered anymore... Rourke keyed the ignition and drove off and dialed his son's cell phone.

Michael Rourke listened before asking, "Dad, are you sure about this?"

"No son, I'm not. But it is reasonable that Jose Zima's thoughts are correct," he said. "Trouble is, there is only one to find out and that is to go there and see."

"I agree it could be important," Michael said, maybe even invaluable. Particularly if the President's Book is real and still exists."

John Rourke nodded, "Could fill in a lot of blanks, that's for sure."

"I'm not sure I can support your plan. This could be pretty tricky, even dangerous."

"Could be," John admitted. "But I think the benefits could outweigh the problems. Remember, we didn't even have the possibility until ten days ago— very little chance of something leaking out. I think with the right equipment and men, this could be pulled off. At least we'd know for sure if there is any basis to the conspiracy between the Russians and the KI or the Russians and the Aliens."

"What if it is both? Michael asked. "What if the Russians we know about are working with the KI? And what if you're correct that there is a Russian faction we're not aware of working with the Aliens?"

"That son, is exactly my point. We have to find out."

"But your plan is... it bothers me. Are you sure the reclaimed clones can be trusted?"

"Look, I know those men have survived a nightmare. And I'm betting they deserve a chance to prove themselves and this operation is... well it is a little unorthodox. But we could find out once and for all. If they prove themselves, we will have a small dedicated force of fighters I think could go up against any threat. Besides, don't forget the other group I mentioned. I know Wes Sanderson and his men are capable."

"But..." Michael started.

"But nothing," John shook his head. "If we disguise this as an archaeological expedition to reclaim Rushmore, I think it will work. Reality is you can't leave; and while Paul is mobile, his leg is not ready for something like this. Wes' people are, and I think humanity owes something to Akiro Kuriname and his people."

Michael knew he had lost this round.

Chapter Sixty-Two

Suddenly, John realized it had been almost three months since he had heard anything from The Keeper; he was worried. Repeatedly, Rourke had tried to reconnect telepathically; so far without success. After The Keeper returned from traveling among the smaller European tribes and brought back evidence proving someone from the KI had been involved in the massacre—that had been bad enough. Realizing the Russians had also been involved was even worse.

Then when The Keeper returned to his people, he had witnessed more troublesome evidence of Russian influence among his own people. The Keeper had spoken to Rourke through his mental powers. *There is now a militaristic slant that is being imposed by the Captain on our activities. We now have weapons being worn in plain sight, there are escorts for members of the Seneia wherever we go. Excursions to your world can now only be authorized by the Captain. Our leader is in very poor health, John. My estimates are he is within the last days of his life. If I am accurate, the Captain has positioned himself and his force to render massive changes in our culture.*

Rourke had no idea what had transpired or whether or not the KI leader was even still alive. John confirmed to The Keeper that the weapon carried by The Keeper's shuttle pilot was one Rourke recognized. He had seen similar ones carried by Russian forces called Spenatz; the elite Russian assault forces. Rourke believed it was absolutely essential that they maintain their communications and keep those communications secret. He believed The Keeper could be the only hope to get advanced information that could prevent a cataclysm for his people and the free people of Earth.

John explained it had been the aggression of the Russians that destroyed his world over 650 years. Their thirst for power had been unquenchable; their penchant for deceit unimaginable and their ability to be trusted non-existent. He cautioned The Keeper that whatever agreements the Captain had made would not be honored. Rourke felt the Captain was being played by an opponent who had centuries of experience in the art of lies and manipulations. He warned that the Russian goals had not changed since the end of the Second World War.

Their conquests, from time to time, have only served to enslave new peoples who heard what they wanted to hear and made the mistake of believing the Russians were capable of honor and the truth.

The Keeper had not been sure if he would be allowed to return to Earth but thought if it were possible it would take him a couple of days to prepare. The Keeper had quoted Einstein from over 600 years before, "'Reality is merely an illusion, albeit a very persistent one.'" That had been their last contact or communication. Rourke wondered, *Could this be another part of the equation?*

Chapter Sixty-Three

Paul Rubenstein was a much harder sell than Michael Rourke. "Hell no I don't like it," he said as he slammed his hand on the desk top. "Look, I know that Wes Sanderson is solid. But the idea of taking these..." He searched for the word.

John Rourke said, "These clones?"

"Yeah, these clones."

"Paul, every report we have from the doctors say they're fine. The severing of contact with the aliens has been successful. They have been training with Sanderson's men and all of the reports are equally satisfactory."

"Give me another couple of weeks, John," Paul said sadly. "The leg is much better, you need someone to watch your back," he pleaded.

"I don't think we have that much time," Rourke said. He walked to Rubenstein's side of the desk and placed his hand on his old friend's shoulder. "I need you and Randall Walls to cover us. You guys are the ones who first discovered those damnable patterns that identify the Alien movement. You know what to look for; time and time again we've tried to teach it to others. Admittedly, it is starting to work but I need the best form of cover I can get for this. That, unfortunately, happens to be you and Walls."

Paul sagged visibly, "Okay, what do you need from us?"

"Most of the 'heavy' stuff we already have—your equipment can detect any visitors we might encounter. The big thing I'm looking at is the technology available before the Night of the War doesn't exist anymore. I don't know how we'll find the records stored if we find records at all. They could be printed out but they just as easily could be on floppy discs or even microfiche."

"The old microform technology was either on film or paper," Rourke said, "and contained micro reproductions of documents for transmission, storage, reading, and printing. Those images were reduced to about one twenty-fifth of the original document size or smaller. They might be made as positives but I'm figuring they'll be negatives. And they might be as microfilm on reels, aperture cards, or the flat sheets used for microfiche. It could even be on the old micro cards. Those were similar to microfiche, but printed on cardboard rather than photographic film. In any event, we need to be able to read the information."

"So, do you have any idea where I'm going to find that kind of technology today?" Paul asked at a total loss.

"I can only think of one, and it means you're going to have to make a road trip to the mainland," Rourke said with a wry smile.

Paul looked puzzled and then he said, "You don't mean..."

Rourke said simply, "Yes, you have to go back to the Retreat. Here is a list of what I want you to locate and bring back."

Chapter Sixty-Four

On the way back from Rubenstein's, Rourke's mind wandered back to a late night, so long ago, when he and Paul sat in the great room of the Retreat. Their journey there had been long; it had also been fruitless because John had not found Sarah and the children. Paul had been stunned in seeing the Retreat that first time, maybe awed would have been the better word.

He had asked John, "How... how did you find this place? My gosh, how did you pull it all together?"

Rourke had smiled, "I planned ahead Paul. I knew that northeast Georgia boasted several low to medium range mountains and the area was full of caves. In fact, the Spanish explorer Hernando de Soto, searched many of those mountain caves for lost Indian treasure in the mid-1500s. He never found the treasure but, to his credit, he did discover the Mississippi River."

"Anyway, I wanted a place to retreat to if the world went crazy. I knew that east of Atlanta stood the most famous mountain in Georgia, Stone Mountain. It has the largest carved high relief sculpture in the world. It is a Confederate Memorial depicting three Confederate heroes of the Civil War: President Jefferson Davis, Generals Robert E. Lee, and Thomas J. 'Stonewall' Jackson."

"A lady named Mrs. C. Helen Plane conceived the idea in 1912. She was a charter member of the United Daughters of the Confederacy or UDC. In 1916, a family named Venable owned the mountain, and deeded the north face of the mountain to the UDC for the memorial. It should have been finished twelve years later but wasn't. In 1963 a guy named Walker Hancock was chosen to complete the carving. Using a new technique utilizing thermo-jet torches to carve away the granite, tons of stone were removed in one day. That technique allowed for fine details with eyebrows, fingers, buckles, and even strands of hair carved with a small thermo-jet torch. The dedication ceremony for the Confederate Memorial Carving was held on May 9, 1970. Finishing touches to the masterpiece were completed in 1972." It is a little over eighty miles from the Retreat to Stone Mountain.

Rourke told Paul, "Before we moved to Georgia I had explored the area, learned the history, and decided this would be the perfect location. On one trip I noticed a very distinctive mountain looming off to my right. It wasn't the tallest mountain in Georgia but, it was just different. Close to its base was the last paved road—Chambers Road. I turned onto a gravel road and about halfway up I got out and explored on foot. It just called out to me as the perfect place for the location of the Retreat. A friend of mine named Steve Fishman was familiar with the area; he thought it was probable there were caves in the area."

"I contacted several geologists and following their suggestions I discovered the entrance to a cave by accident. It was late fall; all of the foliage was dead. I must have walked past it twenty times and never saw it. That day and at that particular time, I saw the hole. I got my bearings and the next day I came back with a set of ropes and a flashlight. I crawled in; it was incredible. I eventually enlarged the opening and put in a system of counter weights. The point is, once I knew there was a cave system honeycombing it, I bought the mountain and the farm."

"I spent years renovating and supplying my hideaway. I hoped I would never need the Retreat but logic dictated it was a good idea anyway. In the end, my preparations proved not to be in vain. Unfortunately, the end did come. Fortunately, I had prepared for it and as a result... well, Paul, you know the rest of the story."

That is where Paul would find the micro technology he and Rourke would probably need to decipher the records stored in Mount Rushmore. That is, if they did in fact exist.

Chapter Sixty-Five

The next morning John Rourke drove to the training site. Chief Warrant Officer Wes Sanderson met him at the gate. "Morning Sir." Sanderson snapped a salute.

"Morning Wes," John, even though he held military rank had never been comfortable with returning salutes; instead he stuck out his hand. "How's the training going?"

"Honestly John they are ahead of schedule. Well ahead." Sanderson led the way over to a Quonset hut-like structure and held the door open for Rourke. "The team leaders will be here in a few minutes. They're finishing up an exercise; want some coffee?"

"Sure. You're satisfied with their progress then I take it."

"Absolutely, they listen and they learn quickly. Physically they are all in top shape and they are anxious to prove themselves; to you and to themselves."

"While we're waiting, tell me what you have gone over with them."

"I started off with basic weapons and tactics. The normal physical conditioning was not really a high priority being they are in good shape. Next—explosives, heavy weapons, repelling, and special warfare. Like I said, I have zero complaints. I think they are ready for about anything we can throw at them."

"How about cold weather training and mountain warfare?"

"They have the basics down pretty well. We just finished a two-week course dealing with operating at altitude, skiing, and mountaineering."

"Are they ready for a real operation?" Rourke asked.

Sanderson stood for a moment, finally saying, "Depends on the mission. You have something in the mix already, don't you?"

"I do, but I'm looking at you to verify they are ready." Rourke took the offered coffee mug and blew on it before taking a sip. Squinting he looked over at Sanderson. "Damn, you guys really drink this mud?"

"Marine mud, Marine coffee. It's the breakfast of champions," Sanderson said with a smile. "We use old socks as filters," he lied.

Rourke smiled, "Tastes like someone has hoof and mouth disease."

Just then a heavy knock on the front door sounded. "Come in," Sanderson called. A dirty mud-stained Akiro Kuriname opened the door and looked in; a smile creased his dirty face.

"John," he said happily running to Rourke. He stopped, dipped his head in a short bow and they shook hands. "I thought you had forgotten about us here."

Rourke smiled, "No Akiro; in fact with Chief Sanderson's and your approval... I think we have an interesting first mission for you and your men."

"Excellent," Kuriname beamed. "What is it?"

"Salvage job, I think. If everything goes well then that is all it should be. We're doing it under the guise of an archaeological expedition."

"But that is just the cover story, I presume." Kuriname smiled. "What is the real treasure we're trying to salvage?"

Rourke turned to Sanderson, "Wes, I have some packages in the backseat of my vehicle. Could you have someone bring them in and sit them on that table in the corner? Also, I need your big screen computer and television and an easel for a flip chart."

"I have my team leaders outside; is it alright for them to sit in on the briefing?" Kuriname asked. "I'll have them bring in your packages."

Rourke looked at Sanderson who just gave a slight nod, "That will be fine, Akiro. As soon as I put everything together, we'll get started."

Chapter Sixty-Six

Paul and the kids were driving the last few miles to the Retreat. His son, John Michael, and his nephews Timothy and John Paul had been excited to make the trip with him. It had been years since they had last seen the Retreat. The flight from Honolulu had been a long one; the boys slept most of the time. After landing in Atlanta, they had not shut up. They had been offered a driver but Paul had turned that offer down. The location of the Retreat at one time had been common knowledge to the general public. Following their first awakening, the Rourke's discovered the Retreat had been a tourist attraction and memorial to the "Heroes of Mankind."

John was able to regain control of the property and when the second sleep occurred, knowledge of the Retreat's location had slipped by the second awakening.

The sheer volume of materials had been impossible to relocate, plus... there was always the fact that the original Retreat could, in fact, be needed yet again. As a stop-gap, he had established a second hideaway in Hawaii. Not as elaborate as the first, but well stocked and geared to immediate survival. In other words, he had simply planned ahead.

John Rourke's second idea for this "mission" was simple, "It's time the guys really got to know the Retreat, Paul. Hopefully, it has served its purpose. However, I think it would be a good time to bring them up-to-speed in case it is ever needed again."

Paul pulled off onto Chambers Road. "Won't be long now guys, as soon as we hit the gravel road we'll be just a few minutes out." Fifteen minutes later, he pulled to the shoulder of the road and said, "Okay, we walk from here. I want each of you to pay attention—just in case you ever have to come here without me or your dads."

Twenty minutes later Paul eyed the familiar landmarks. "We're here." The guys looked around confused.

"Where? I don't see anything," Timothy finally said.

Paul laughed, "That's what I said the first time your dad brought me here. He told me, 'You're not supposed to see anything.' Come over here." They were about halfway up the mountainside; he walked to a large boulder on the right and pushed against it with his hands. The boulder rolled away; he walked to his far left where a similar, but squared-off rock butted against the granite face.

"Watch," Paul said pushing on it. "John did a lot of research in archeology to come up with this system." He braced himself against the rock and pushed it aside. There was rumbling in the rock itself; the boys drew back. The rock on which Paul stood began to sink and, as it did, a slab of rock about the size of a single-car-garage door began to slide inward. "John said it's just weights and counterbalances. If you want to open from inside, levers perform the same function as moving the rocks out here."

The boys leaned forward, trying to see into the open doorway and the darkness beyond. "Come on," Paul said, walking into the darkness. "Tim, there's a red handled lever in there, by the light switch. Swing it down and lock it under the notch."

"Got it."

Paul bent down and rolled the two rock counterbalances into position, then stepped into the cave. He bent to the red handled lever, loosed it safely from the notch and raised it; the granite doorway started to move, the rock beneath them shuddering audibly. He flipped a hidden switch and light filled the area. *Electricity, thanks to the stream,* Paul thought. Before them stood steel double doors at the far end of the antechamber. Paul walked to the steel doors and began spinning a combination dial. He then pushed the lever-shaped handles; the doors swung open.

"Tim," Paul said, walking into the darkness, "kill that light switch for red back there, okay?" Ten seconds later he whispered "Now," and hit the light switch.

"Wow!" John Michael whispered as Paul smiled and stepped down into the great room.

"Just like we left it," Paul said as he looked around. "That is a good thing. Come on." The boys were as quiet as if they were in church. There was a

166

natural rock wall separating the chamber they were in from the main cavern and there were rows upon rows of shelves on it, stacked floor to ceiling and several large ladders.

Pointing, Paul said, "Over there is spare ammunition plus some reloading components. Over there is food, whiskey, whatever. Over there is toilet paper, paper towels, bath soap, shampoo and conditioner, candles, light bulbs— sixties, hundreds, fluorescent tubes—light switches, screws, nails, bolts, nuts, washers. Chain saws and hand saws. Over there is the main supply of ammunition." There were spaces for .22 Long Rifle, .38 Special, .357 Magnum, 9mm, .44 Magnum, and .45 ACP, then the rifle cartridges .223 and .308, then 12-gauge shotgun shells, double 0 buck and rifled slugs. "John told me, 'mostly two and three-quarter-inch because it works in the three-inch Magnums, but not vice-versa.'"

Paul showed them row upon row of Mountain House foods in large containers and small packages, ordinary canned goods and other food supplies, then stacks of white boot socks, underpants, and handkerchiefs. A large bin at one end of the shelving area held holsters, slings, and various other leather goods. Beyond this was a shelf filled with a dozen pair of black GI combat boots, and beside them a half dozen pairs of rubber thongs.

He pointed out a truck. "It's a Ford, four-wheel-drive pickup; John converted it to run off pure ethyl alcohol. There's a distillery for it set up on the far side over there." Paul walked back to the end of the shelf row and hit one switch and the side cavern behind them went dark. He hit a second switch and the darkened smaller chamber ahead of them illuminated. "Work room," and pointed along the walls and down a row of long tables. Vises, reloading equipment, power saws, drill press; then, ranked on shelves above these were oil filters, spark plugs, fan belts—tools hung on pegboard wall panels beyond them.

The complete tour took over two hours with explanations; and, in some cases, demonstrations. Finally Paul said, "Okay, we sleep here tonight. Let's get some grub and showers. Tomorrow we have a full day. It won't be a problem to find the equipment but I want to run some checks to be sure it still works and it will probably take a couple of loads to get it all." *The boys haven't said five words between themselves since the tour started,* Paul thought. He remembered his first exposure to the Retreat, and smiled. The boys sat up all night, Paul could hear them talking but couldn't make out the conversations.

The next morning he was up before them and had breakfast ready when they finally rolled out of bed. John Paul was the first to get up, "Uncle Paul, we talked last night and I've got a question."

"Shoot."

"The Retreat, Uncle Paul," he said with a hesitation. "It seems smaller somehow than any of us remember. I mean it is still impressive but are we all nuts or did it shrink somehow?"

Paul laughed, "You are too much like your grandfather and nothing gets passed you." At that time the other two came in. Paul said, "Listen you guys, it didn't shrink... you got bigger. Come over here and take a look." The boys followed, "John made these marks on the wall the last time all three of you were here together. They show how tall each of you were then."

"Man, we were little. I didn't think it was that long ago," John Michael said.

Paul smiled, "It's only been a few years guys but each of you has definitely grown. Now get over there and finish your breakfast. We have work to do and..." Shifting into what could only be called a Jewish imitation of John Wayne, Paul said, "... we're burnin' day light."

*****

It took two days before "the crew," as the boys referred to themselves, landed back in Honolulu. With them were four large cases including a microfiche reader, a word processor that read floppy disks, an ancient slide projector, a reel-to-reel tape recorder and some assorted other devices; and, a very exhausted Paul Rubenstein in tow. Paul called John Rourke, "Okay, we're home. Yeah, the guys had a great time. I can't be sure but I think we have everything you will need."

"Excellent," John said. "Get with Randall Walls this evening; I want you guys to start watching the area now for those patterns. Mission goes in three days."

168

Chapter Sixty-Seven

At Sanderson's insistence, John was back at the Dog Soldier's training site, "Thought you might like to watch this John." Sanderson led the way to the base of the cliff which was several hundred feet high. Rourke could see lines of rope descending from the top with men sliding down on harnesses. Calls of "On Repel" were followed by an answering, "On Belay." Sanderson turned off the ATV and they watched as the clone warriors descended over 200 feet down the cliff face. A scream cut the morning stillness. Rourke watched helplessly as one warrior apparently lost footing at the crest of the descent. The man slid straight down the rope with both hands maintaining a death grip on that life-line; it appeared his foot hit an outcropping that flipped him inverted. The thump of his head hitting against the rock face was audible; he slammed into the next man below him on the rope knocking him loose and sending both tumbling toward the rocky base of the cliff, both slamming several times into the rock face.

Below, Sanderson's Special Operator, the belay man for that rope, had instantly thrown his entire body weight on the rope, pulling it taught. Even with his fast reaction, it was still just yards short of impact before the two men on the rope stopped their deadly slide.

An eerie quiet settled over the scene only to be interrupted by a bull horn that ordered, "Lock it up in place!" Several other operators on the ground as observers ran to the effected line and movement ceased on the other lines; belay men below dropped their weight against the lines. Slowly, the two injured men were lowered to the ground, bloodied and unconscious; Rourke, Sanderson and a Medic ran over. The men were lowered to the ground slowly, the Locking D rings and Figure eight devices were removed, and they were stretched as flat and gently as possible on the ground. The Medic arrived first and did a quick assessment.

Slowly he turned to Sanderson, "These two are done for right now." Slowly one man regained consciousness but the other lay still and unmoving. "Williams is out, we need to get him to the hospital; his helmet is cracked and he's bleeding from the scalp, ears and nose. He has at least a concussion, maybe a skull fracture or worse," the Medic said. "A compound fracture of the right forearm on Billings here. Give me a minute or two and get the ambulance up here."

While two of the Spec Ops personnel worked on Billings to secure his arm, the Medic placed a cervical collar on Williams. Rourke and Sanderson helped keep his spine and neck straight as the unconscious man was rolled up slightly on one side to allow a back board to be slid under him. Velcro straps were adjusted to hold his head and body in position for transport just as the ambulance dry skidded to a halt near them. "I'll ride in the bus with him, bring Billings on the next one," the Medic said. "I've got to get X-rays on both men before I can give you a report."

On top of the cliff face the remaining Dog Soldiers stood, knelt, or laid flat looking down over the edge at the tabloid of events playing out below them; wondering if the men had survived and thankful they had not been the ones who fell. Conversation was in hushed tones and concern for their comrades was evident on their faces. That is except in the face of one; no one noticed the slight smile twisting his lips as he stood and walked away from the edge to stand alone.

That was simple enough, he thought.

Chapter Sixty-Eight

Sanderson and Rourke were sitting in the waiting area when the doctor came out of x-ray. He called them into a consultation room and placed the two sets of x-rays on the lighted viewing panels. Quietly he studied both, shook his head and turned to Sanderson, "Chief, you're going to be down two men for some time. Billings I'm not too worried about—fracture of the radius and the ulna. The radial break is a compound. We won't know anything until I have it repaired; if there is no nerve damage resulting from the bone ripping through the muscles and nerves, he'll be okay in a few weeks. If there's nerve damage... well, I just don't know yet."

"What about Williams?" Sanderson asked.

"He's going to be down for some time. Take a look," the doctor said pointing at one set of x-rays. "Cervical fracture on two vertebrae, plus a skull fracture here. Of the two, it's the cervical fractures I'm most concerned about; it is possible the spinal cord is compromised. Both men are being prepped for surgery as we speak. I'll let you know something as soon as we can get inside and take a look." The doctor turned and headed out to scrub up.

Chapter Sixty-Nine

Dr. Karen Cummings, taller than most women, a little over 5 feet 9 inches, was slender though not skinny and carried herself with confidence and bearing. President Michael Rourke had tasked her with the responsibility of setting up the meeting. At the conference table sat several high ranking military officers and a smattering of scientists. The President, John Rourke, Wes Sanderson, and Akiro Kuriname were there. She approached the conference table and waited. As the attendees settled down she said, "Hello, I'm Dr. Karen Cummings. My Ph.D. is in ice age studies, which means I have studied climate change in order to explain the colossal coming and going of ice ages. There are several methods and ingenious techniques to recover evidence from the distant past; first from deposits left on land, then from sea floor sediments and then still better by drilling deep into ice."

Rourke smiled. "I guess you could be called an 'iceologist?'"

Dr. Cummings flashed a fetching smile. "Yes, I guess you could call it that. My second Ph.D. is as a paleoclimatologist and that deals with the strangely regular pattern of glacial cycles. The timing of the cycles is set by minor changes in sunlight caused by slow variations of the earth's orbit. Just how that could regulate the ice ages remains uncertain; the climate system turned out to be dauntingly complex. While it is accepted that 'greenhouse' gases, like carbon dioxide, played a surprisingly powerful role in governing global climate, it was not the only consideration. Our climate system is actually rather delicately poised, so that a little stimulus might drive a great change. The use of satellites to monitor the ice at the earth's poles has enabled us to better understand changes in our climate. Now, if you would, I'd like each of you to identify yourself and your specialty as it relates to this meeting."

The introductions took only about five minutes and Dr. Cummings resumed. "Thank you. Now, I compare data from satellites with measurements collected on and inside the ice. Doing experiments in the extreme conditions found on glaciers presents unique problems: equipment failure of generators and radar equipment one of the first. Even getting to the ice can be tough. The area you're talking about routinely has storms with thirty-five mile per hour winds that can be sustained at sixty miles per hour for days at a time."

The next speaker to stand and explain his expertise was the director of the Center for Snow and Avalanche Studies, Frank O'Conner. "At the Center, we study avalanches, what causes them, how to survive being caught in one; and, how if necessary, to create a manmade avalanche."

"I thought it was just when snow and ice dislodged from the side of a mountain and careened down the slope," Rourke said.

"In the basic application you are correct. Normally an avalanche occurs when the snow-packed layers of accumulated snow on the side of a mountain are in some way disturbed, leading to a fracturing of the top layer and a downward torrent of a large mass of the white stuff."

One of the military officers asked, "What sets off the disturbance?"

"A number of factors can set off a disturbance," O'Conner said. "They include natural factors like new precipitation, which could be rain or additional snow, a sudden warming, wind, ice fall or rock fall, as well as so-called artificial factors like skiers and snowmobilers. The long-held notion that avalanches can be triggered by the human voice has been largely debunked. Our studies show that ninety percent of avalanche fatalities are triggered by the weight of one of the victims in the group. In other words, the pressure exerted by human movement caused a fracture in the snowpack, loosening the top layer and unleashing a torrent of snow. Most avalanches occur twenty-four hours after a rapid, heavy snowfall."

Sanderson raised his hand, "You're saying there is more than one kind of avalanche?"

"Actually, there are two main types. A 'loose snow avalanche' typically occurs on steep terrain and is a teardrop-shaped mass that gathers volume and intensity as it travels down the mountain. A loose snow avalanche usually occurs with freshly fallen, low-density snow or old snow that's been softened by extended sunlight."

"The second type is a 'slab avalanche,' in which a layer of snow separates, shatters like glass and comes hurtling down a mountain. Slab avalanches account for about ninety percent of avalanche deaths. As I understand the mission parameters, this is the kind you want to create to accomplish your mission. What you're basically looking at is the artificial process called calving. An example would be when a glacier close to the water calves and an iceberg is created."

"There are several factors in the calving process. These are longitudinal stretching, often this forms crevasses. If the crevasse penetrates the full thickness of the ice, calving will occur. Normally, longitudinal stretching is controlled by friction at the base and edges of the glacier, glacier geometry and water pressure at the bed."

"And you believe it is possible to artificially induce that type stretching?" Rourke asked.

"Absolutely, it is essential. Otherwise you risk damaging the busts carved on the mountain itself. While they haven't been seen in hundreds of years, their destruction from the use of high explosives would be unconscionable."

Cummings raised her hand. "Let me do some core sampling and figure out the construction of the ice. Coupling that with what we know about Mount Rushmore, I believe we can give a safe method to slide the ice and snow right off of it."

Another military officer asked, "Exactly how do you intend to accomplish that?"

Cummings, now focused, flipped on the computer screen, "As you can see, if we can use a pinpoint application of directed heat and sound vibration, it will work. We can use microwave transmissions to create a thin layer of disturbance deep in the ice. Controlled concussive sound should slide it right off."

"How long would you estimate your analysis and abatement would take?" Rourke asked.

"With the right equipment and weather conditions, one to two days— no more."

"And you have the equipment you need?"

"Some of it is out in the field on another survey. If you say it is a go, it can be on site within forty-eight hours."

Sanderson's team and the Dog Soldier group's training had dealt with conditions such as terrain and weather, techniques of military mountaineering, operations on glaciers and snow covered mountains.

After glancing at his notes Sanderson said, "With Mount Rushmore at a height of just under 5,800 feet, it might be a little uncomfortable but won't involve the problems on mountain real estate with an altitude of 10,000 to 23,000 feet. Today's military has no experience fighting in truly high mountains. We have several archived mountain warfare manuals that deal primarily with low and medium mountains and stress the use of helicopter aviation to conduct that combat. However, helicopters cannot haul normal loads over 13,000 feet. Above that the rotors lack thick enough air to 'bite' into. Also, altitude sickness will not be a concern during this operation."

Kuriname then jumped in explaining more details concerning the upcoming operation. "Our teams will set up security for the scientists. Under the cover that this is an attempt to restore one of America's national treasures, it should be a simple operation. We'll be there to supplement the scientists. Once the ice covering has been dealt with, we'll explore the immediate area with ultrasonic equipment and locate the Hall of Records. If the door to it is inoperable, and we're figuring after centuries under the ice it will be, we will use plasma cutters to remove the artifacts and records."

"The scientists will examine them immediately; if in their opinion we have found what we are hoping to find, we'll transport them back here. Centuries under the ice and what that has done to the records is a big concern. We're hoping it won't be necessary to use extraordinary conservation techniques but we are equipped for that eventuality. On the short side, once the ice is gone, in less than twenty-four hours, we'll be back in the air headed home. Worse case, if heavy conservation is required before transport... an additional twenty-four to thirty-six hours."

"Okay Wes, you know my next question..." Rourke said.

"Yes sir, I do," Sanderson said looking at Kuriname. "These men are ready and my men are ready."

"You both realize we're not sure what condition Mount Rushmore is in or the artifacts stored there. Of primary interest is the recovery of the documents and artifacts. My biggest concern is the condition of any paper documentation. The acid paper commonly used before the Night of the War is notorious for disintegrating over time; especially this length of time. We'll have several paper conservators assigned to assess its condition at the site. I hate to say this but Mount Rushmore has not been seen in several hundred years. While I want us to do everything in our power to restore it, don't forget the mission."

"John, we understand," Kuriname assured. "Chief Sanderson and I are in agreement. Especially since our cover story is we are on an archeological expedition, we have to successfully remove the ice and snow. That, in and of itself, will restore the monument."

Rourke nodded, "I hope so but the mission comes first; the restoration is a secondary concern."

Chapter Seventy

Michael stood tall as he addressed the joint chambers of Congress. "President Theodore Roosevelt talked about war. He said, 'War is an ugly thing, but not the ugliest of things. The decayed and degraded state of moral and patriotic feeling, which that nothing is worth war, is much worse. A man who has nothing for which he is willing to fight, nothing he cares for more than his personal safety is a miserable creature who has no chance of being free unless made and kept that way by the exertions of better men than himself.'"

"There is a plan to bring down societies of free people; in a variety of forms it has existed for quite some time. It is the same plan that was established to give socialists the opportunity to take a society into communism. You can see for yourself how many of these have already been accomplished. First was the control of healthcare; if you control healthcare you control the people."

"The second was to increase the poverty level as high as possible; poor people are easier to control and will not fight back if you are providing everything for them to live. Next is to increase the debt to an unsustainable level; that way you are able to increase taxes, and this will produce more poverty. Gun control efforts are not truly based in safety and security concerns. Its goal is to remove the ability to defend themselves from the Government. That way you are able to create a police state."

"Welfare had to increase; this would allow the government to take control of every aspect of citizens' lives; their food, housing, and their income. If you control the education system you are able to take control of what people read and listen to. Take control of what children learn in school; over only one generation, the dream of a nation can change."

"It was essential to remove the name of God from the Government and schools. And finally, institute a policy of class warfare. You must divide the people into the wealthy and the poor. This will cause more discontent and it will be easier to take, through taxes, the wealthy with the support of the poor."

Sitting in the audience and somewhat distracted, John Rourke suddenly realized how proud he was of his son Michael; but he knew Michael was growing tired of the political... 'bull shit' was the only term that came to mind. John's was a world that required more actions and fewer words. Michael had accomplished something amazing to Rourke; he thrived on the political nuisances. It seemed he had finally found his niche. He had also had the benefit of his stepfather, Wolfgang Mann, who had tutored Michael in some of those finer nuisances of politics. John thought to himself, *it really paid off.* Like Mann, Michael had successfully made the transformation from John's world to those "hallowed halls."

Michael had wedded two distinct arenas—politics and patriotism—into one... his presidency. John on the other hand was ready for some action. Michael spoke again, "History is replete with incidents where the very same measure the Progressives promote have not only been ineffective, but have resulted in complete financial ruin for countless countries over the centuries. You can't tax your way back from the precipice on which we stand. Help from the government... I agree we must help; we must help create jobs. We must give a hand up not a hand out; that plan throughout history has destroyed personal initiative and self-reliance."

"Cicero said, and I quote, 'A nation can survive its fools, and even the ambitious. But it cannot survive treason from within. An enemy at the gates is less formidable, for he is known and carries his banner openly. But the traitor moves amongst those within the gate freely, his sly whispers rustling through all the alleys, heard in the very halls of government itself. For the traitor appears not a traitor; he speaks in accents familiar to his victims, and he wears their face and their arguments, he appeals to the baseness that lies deep in the hearts of all men. He rots the soul of a nation, he works secretly and unknown in the night to undermine the pillars of the city, he infects the body politic so that it can no longer resist. A murderer is less to fear.'"

"The traitor is the culprit we must focus on. Otherwise, nothing else we do, nothing else we accomplish, will have any lasting effect," Michael said with a steely gaze. "The traitor is who we are focusing on. Additionally, let me say that one of his tools has always been the need for more political correctness. I will tell you, this world had political correctness before the Night of the War and I experienced it. I have studied it and I find directions are creating a trend I find troubling. I understand why there are a lot of people who sincerely believe that changes were necessary and appropriate. However, as with the current political processes in this country, 'change' took on a life of its own while remaining surprisingly ill-defined and irresponsible with its own consequences."

Chapter Seventy-One

Michael Rourke's last visit to New Germany had been months ago. Now, yet again he saw that the season was changing; he had enjoyed the visit on the last night with his mother Sarah. Even though she had come to help with the kids after Natalia's injuries, it seemed like it had been too long between visits.

Michael and Wolfgang Mann, president of New Germany, had coordinated on this summit. The scientific leaders of the New World were gathered in the Rotunda at the New German Capital. Mann opened the meeting, "Gentlemen, we are gathered here to discuss a global crisis. We have evidence of a threat, actually coming at us from several directions that will potentially affect all of us. We have found evidence, an unsubstantiated report, that the aliens made contact with the German government in 1933. During the 1930's, the Germans had been building rockets and there was even talk about a space program. Plans for weapons such as sound devices, lasers, neutron bombs, particle beam weapons, etc., were designed. Although many of these weapons were not created until much later in history, apparently there was an exchange of technology that was shared with the Germans such as anti-gravity and free energy."

"There is another, equally unconfirmed report, that the Roswell incident was supposedly not a crash but rather a shoot down. Supposedly the U.S. government, using a military radar system, targeted and brought down the craft. Another report says the United States Government made a formal agreement with an alien race in a meeting at Holliman Air Force Base in 1954. The terms of this agreement were the exchange of technology, of anti-gravity, metals, alloys, and environmental technologies to assist the earth with free energy, and medical application regarding the human body."

He turned to Michael, "Mr. President..."

Michael looked at the audience and said, "In exchange the aliens would be allowed to study the human development, both in the emotional consciousness makeup, and to reside here on earth. That particular document and original exchange material was supposedly stored in a NSA facility, called Blue Moon, under Kirkland Air Force Base in New Mexico. If that report was ever accurate information, proof has been lost. We can't confirm any of it. The Night of the War destroyed a lot of documents and artifacts. If anything was ever stored in Blue Moon, it isn't now. However, the alien agenda now is apparently to create a slave race that can mine this world for resources. We suspect that there has been extensive research on the human brain and its capabilities. For decades before the Night of the War, there were many people who claim to have been abducted and even implanted by the aliens."

"We now know the aliens are capable of monitoring the brain waves of those they have cloned, through the tattoos. The clones lost free will, they were little more than clone robots! Their souls were trapped and they were no longer considered compassionate human beings. They're trapped mentally, emotionally, physically in a physical existence, therefore, that's all they see. They literally disowned and fractionalized themselves away from their spiritual essence. That type of control is now no longer a part of them."

"Supposedly, in the late 1950's, the aliens allegedly also approached the Russians regarding the signing of treaties and mutual exchange. The Russians, however, chose not to sign this independent treaty because they knew full well that the aliens would try to pit the United States against the Soviet Union. It is in fact the Soviet Union that informed President John F. Kennedy of the alien presence during the Cuban missile crisis."

Mann spoke again, "Apparently, after the Night of the War, whatever contact the aliens had with this planet was either stopped or simply went unnoticed. However, interviewing those rescued members of the clones from the Eden Project, we now know the threat is real."

David Hawk, the Minister of Science for England interrupted, "Mr. Rourke, you are saying we have indisputable facts that a global threat is imminent?"

"Yes Minister, we do. And at least part of that threat is not external to our atmosphere. We now believe the plan is to have us morally and spiritually compromise our free will—they let us create the destruction to ourselves. It really is a set-up. The power of belief systems can be used as fuel for the game of seducing people into believing that certain things are true. By the power created by the conscious thoughts, we can literally make these things occur and come true, whether they benefit us or not. There are real, spiritual dynamics at work here and they're being used against us."

Michael continued, "Certainly, anything is possible. We have to focus on what we can do. We, of Earth, have evolved only in technical and material sciences. My fear is that there is a covert plan for a New World Order. It could be that the population of the Earth could be seduced. If a billion people come to the realization and a decision that it is safer, more reasonable, more politically correct to capitulate, it can literally change with the setting and the rising of the sun. I stress, this threat has many angles. We are not just dealing with an external enemy. We believe that the promise of a 'shared domination' of the world has already been made. Individual and collective greed on the part of traitors... traitors not only to our individual nations, but traitors to the human race are involved."

A dark man stood; he spoke with a heavy Spanish accent, "You are saying that if subtle manipulation does not work, force will be levied against us. If these evil powers are not able to manipulate our belief system level, there is also a plan in development to play out a staged second coming of the threat. This apparently has already begun with the arrival of the KI. Are they part of this?"

Michael hesitated, "I don't believe that all of the KI would be involved in this. However, evidence is being presented that some might be willing to change the course of human history in conjunction with a more militant segment of their population. We suspect some sort of an alliance is being, or has been, forged with a secret Russian facility and there appear to be elements of advancement being introduced that we cannot copy. Mankind has developed significantly from our early ancestors, particularly in the area of arms and armaments. In a direct confrontation, the militant KI can't take over without risking their own safety."

David Hawk stood and turned to the rest of the scientific leaders. He slowly turned back to Rourke. "So... Mr. Rourke. What do you need from us?"

"We need some serious brain power and coordination but, more than that, it is essential you understand the overall view. This meeting was called to review the apparent intent and the effects of the actions of the aliens and the traitorous humans. We now can confirm that after Earth's climatic and geological calamity

40,000 years ago, members of the KI race were stranded here. They kept their identity secret and integrated with those cultures that survived. From all indications they DID form the basis for many, if not all, of our legends and heroic stories from every corner of the planet. Their race was longer lived than the proto-humans and their life span allowed them interaction for several generations. We think it is entirely possible that they, or the memories our proto-humans ancestors had of them, were the nugget of truth in our mythological gods and goddesses."

"What our ancestors did not have the technology to explain became the magic of the gods. For several generations of human development, the influence of the surviving KI guided and influenced the growth from barbaric hunter gathers through the development of agriculture and the establishment of villages. Eventually, those KI did die off. The memories of them became enshrouded in myths and legends. Almost all of these memories carried a similar message that one day, the 'gods' would return."

"As you know, they have," Mann said. "However, now that the KI have returned, we have information there is a faction within them that has become... I guess militarized is the appropriate term; that faction wants to take the control of Earth away from present day humans and the other returnees. While there are elements of their sciences and technology we don't yet understand, we know they have limits not exceptionally different from our own. First, the entire KI population of returnees is, by comparison to the population of Earth, small in numbers. Secondly, while there are elements of advancement we cannot copy, we are stronger than our earlier ancestors which they were familiar with."

David Hawks said, "But you said there is some type of alliance between humans and KI that could be successful?"

Michael nodded. "Yes, but it is the wrong group of humans who have aligned. Specifically, a temporary alliance between them and a hidden Russian outpost appears to have already occurred. I believe the Russian plan is to gain knowledge of KI technology and use their sciences, their ships, and their people to assist the Russians in gaining dominance over the world. Then the Russians will turn on the KI and place them under their global fist of control."

"We now have reports of several incidents and activities we believe are evidence of such an alliance. And we have confirmation from within the KI themselves of the appearance of Russian weaponry on the KI ships. There have been several 'suspicious' events that have occurred in a general sequence and timeline that unfolded at several sites and locations around the globe. This operational plan we're passing out will provide an overview of what happened at each location and when."

"I hope it will useful to analyze the effectiveness of any anticipated responses we may have to take; especially the time-sensitive actions. We need to brainstorm a means of looking at the ramifications of one action not happening when expected, on actions taken by other players and on the overall response; otherwise... we won't be successful."

Chapter Seventy-Two

The team consisted of the ten scientists assigned to Dr. Cummings and Frank O'Conner, the members of Akiro Kuriname's Dog Soldiers, Wes Sanderson's special warfare unit, and John Rourke. Randall Walls and Paul Rubenstein tapped into surveillance satellites and were monitoring the entire northern part of North America for signs the mission had been compromised.

Transport near to the site, formally known as Mount Rushmore, had been accomplished by the huge VTOL transport planes. From there it was a mile over land, more accurately an over glacier trip, in Vikings which was the snowmobile version of the All-Terrain Powered Armored Attack Vehicles. Camp was set up the first day and the scientists had set up the equipment they would need. Four hours later, the exact location of the faces of Mount Rushmore had been determined and sensors were deployed to determine the exact pattern of frequency modulation necessary to "de-ice" the monument and give them access to the Hall of Records.

Chief Sanderson and Akiro Kuriname were in their tent. "Wes, I have an uneasy feeling about this mission," Kuriname said.

"Really Akiro, it seems to be a simple salvage operation," Sanderson said.

Kuriname nodded, "I agree but I can't shake this feeling. Something is 'out of sequence' and I can't figure out what it is."

"Look," Sanderson said, "this is the first operation for your team. Heebie-jeebies are to be expected. Your guys will do fine and so will you."

"I need your help," Kuriname said after a long silence. "I'm concerned about one of my men, Bennett Arnold. He just seems... I can't put my finger on it. He seems different, distant somehow. Will you help me watch him? I really want this first mission to go well."

"Sure," Sanderson said. "I don't know what you mean though, he seems fine to me."

"I don't know what, but..." Akiro said, "something just doesn't feel right where he is concerned. I agree it could be nothing more than pre-operations nerves. But help me watch him."

"Will do."

Chapter Seventy-Three

Dr. Cummings consulted with Frank O'Conner, "Here are the readings and our extrapolations, Frank. Do you agree?"

Studying the reports, O'Conner pushed his glass up on his forehead. "Yes, I agree. At those angles I believe you can set up an area of disturbance. By my calculations, after thirty minutes of stimulation, if the ice has not started to slide, we can initiate sonic concussive blasts with the ultrasonic cannons here, here and here. That should dislodge the ice face."

Cummings studied the computer model, after several seconds she said, "Then we initiate now," and flipped a switch. The microwave generators hummed as their power was increased. "Start the time clock."

Sanderson and Kuriname's men had established over watch security for the entire operation one half mile back from the affected zone. They were monitoring the air space above them and staying in contact with Paul Rubenstein and Walls who were monitoring the entire northern hemisphere above the continental U.S.; so far everything was going as planned.

Twenty-five minutes after the microwave transmitters were activated there were no signs of activity. At twenty-seven minutes, thirty seconds, the first fissures began opening in the glacial covering. O'Conner said, "Now! Hit the sonic cannons." Deep, thumping sounds were directed toward the ice and snow on both sides of the monument and were felt, more than heard, by the scientists. The ice coverings on the monument faces had to be simultaneously destroyed for a successful archaeological mission. But, they also had to clear the ice from the top of the monument and the back slope to accomplish their real mission—access to the Hall of Records.

The slippage of hundreds of years of snow and ice accumulation had to be precise or the Mount Rushmore monument and the Hall of Records could both be destroyed. O'Conner studied the snow, "Kick it up another five decibels please." One of the technicians dialed in the corrections—the fissures widened.

"Alright, mount up!" O'Conner ordered. "We have to leave here right now." He knew he was probably sacrificing hundreds of thousands of dollars of equipment but it couldn't be helped. The concussive waves had to continue but he would not ask anyone to stay behind to operate the equipment.

Chapter Seventy-Four

The slides started minutes later; thousands of metric tons of ice and snow which accumulated over 650 years, shivered. Fissures opened from mere inches to several feet and then yards. Suddenly, there was a cacophony of sound and force on both sides of the crest of Mount Rushmore. In front, the busts of presidents shown through with just a microscopically thin layer of water generated by the microwave generators that provided the lubrication. The concussive cannons provided the kinetic energy. The roar of falling ice and snow was deafening.

Rourke watched the monitors and then looked down the slope. For the first time in centuries, four presidential faces shown in the morning light. Darker than Rourke remembered, *I hope that is just the water layer*, he thought. Turning to Dr. Cummings, "Okay Doc, looks like this worked. Where is the Hall of Records?"

Sanderson's and Kuriname's teams reformed on the crest of the mountain. Security was the first consideration; scientific discovery a distant second. Setting secure points and attaching repelling ropes, several squads of men descended behind the presidential busts while their compatriots remained on guard. Following their locator devices they moved forward. After moving several feet of debris and ice, the doors stood before them. The doors had stood for centuries, solid and locked as though against the world—against the insanity of it. Electronic lock picking devices opened the doors in less than fifteen minutes. They were inside—Shangri-La!

The conservation technicians examined the storage containers; six had lost structural integrity. Only the universe knew what secrets were lost. The rest appeared to be intact; there was more material than anyone had imaged. A "fire bucket brigade" was formed and the intact containers were moved to the pickup points on the crest of the mountain. That project alone would take several hours.

Chapter Seventy-Five

Three of the ATPAAVs were making constant round trips to the VTOL transport plane over a mile away. Now, the Hall of Records stood empty for the first time in centuries. It had served its purpose with distinction. With the last containers on their way to the transport planes, the operation had moved to a cleanup phase. Two more trips and the last of the scientists and the first of the security teams would be loaded and ready to return home. John Rourke smiled at Sanderson and slapped Akiro on the back, "A double success guys: recovery of the artifacts and successful abatement of centuries of ice and snow from one of our nation's greatest monuments. It is a great day."

"Yes, it is," Kuriname said still unable to shake the sense of foreboding.

At that instant, Rourke's satellite phone cheeped. "Go ahead," was all he said. This phone was on a separate frequency from the others. On the other end was Paul Rubenstein, watching for those "patterns."

Paul advised, "You have incoming! ETA fifteen minutes, maybe ten. Evacuate to the southeast. Rally at Point Victor for extraction. I repeat, Point Victor."

"Roger," Rourke said into the radio. "Damnit! Get everything moving; we have company, inbound. Load everybody up, Wes, contact the VTOLs, tell them to launch and move to Point Victor; we'll meet them there. Any equipment not already loaded on the ATPAAVs; leave it. We have to leave now. Tell your drivers to make it to Point Victor for extraction."

Sanderson and Kuriname nodded and ran off to initiate the orders. Rourke hoped they had time to complete them but he didn't think they would. Rourke watched the loading process and took a last look around; discarded equipment littered the area. Rourke ran to the juncture of the glacier; a Viking slid to a stop next to him, "Get in Mr. Rourke."

"Thanks for the lift, let's move out." The driver stepped on the gas and rocketed across the ice. The other ATPAAVs charged ahead of them. They were already over a half-mile away and leaving them behind. Rourke shouted into the wind, "Go! Go! You have to catch up to them."

Rourke realized the gap to the other Vikings increased; it now stood at about a mile. A hundred yards in front of them, the snow suddenly exploded. Rourke lost sight of the other vehicles; more energy bolts flashed from the sky. The driver swerved to avoid a chasm that opened up in front of them. Hanging on to the overhead roof cage, Rourke turned to his right and looked behind; two silver objects streaked toward them belching green energy bursts. "Turn!" Rourke shouted. "You have to go right damnit and step on it! We have to catch up; the VTOLs won't wait on us."

Suddenly, the vehicle slowed then stopped. Rourke whipped around to see what new danger was stopping them; nothing. He looked incredulously at the driver and shouted, "What the hell?" The driver's left hand held a pistol pointed at Rourke's chest. "I'm counting on the VTOLs not waiting for us, Mr. Rourke." An energy blast hit nearby, throwing snow and ice on them just as Rourke pulled his Sting 1A boot knife and lunged. The driver squeezed the trigger just as the wave of concussion violently rocked the ATPAAV onto its side, throwing both men out.

Rourke rolled through the impact, landing on his back. He scrambled to his feet just as the driver leapt at him; Rourke's left hand closed on the man's throat as the impact sent them rolling. Rourke now on top, his grip tightened; the man's face began turning red. Rourke stabbed at the man's face but his assailant's left hand gripped Rourke's wrist in mid thrust.

Sharp pain suddenly stabbed through Rourke's chest; his strength faded and his grip loosened. The driver coughed violently and shoved Rourke over. Rourke tried to move but couldn't, he thought, *I'm dying.* Looking down he saw a hypodermic sticking out of his chest. Rourke's world started spinning as his attacker stood over him and he noticed the man's name tag for the first time— ARNOLD.

Why? Rourke's mind framed the question silently as darkness took him completely.

Epilogue

Every fiber in Rourke's body was on fire, but he could do nothing. His mind had climbed slowly back to a conscious level and he screamed silently— the scream was locked in his mind. Not a sound came from him. The fire consuming him was total; he wished for death. The pain was so intense. He wished for movement so he could run, but he was keenly aware of the restraints that held him to the hard, unyielding surface. *Feels like an examination table,* he thought. Rourke had no choice but to suffer the agony, silently.

He was mentally aware but physically numbed—unable to move. Bits and pieces of his life flashed through that part of his mind that was conscious. Memories of every injury he sustained came back; every agony he endured flooded over him. None of them came close to the suffering he now endured. Then, as suddenly as the agony had consumed him, it miraculously stopped.

Sweat covered his naked skin. Stink from the sweat threatened to smother him; still, he could not move. Blessedly, he lost consciousness again. The being he knew as The Creator stood over him, expressionless, without Rourke's knowledge.

He awoke again; he opened his eyes. After many minutes, his vision returned. *I'm not blind,* he thought. As he focused, the scene around him could only be described as... alien. He was alone. He had no frames of reference to define where he was. Then it hit him, with the force of a nuclear detonation.

John Thomas Rourke had been captured. He was now in the hands of the greatest enemy the planet Earth had ever faced—The Creator. Fear grabbed him low in the gut, and flushed upward through his chest. The first sound he made erupted from his mouth—a single scream that encompassed more fear, more dread, more hopeless than he had ever felt.

His right hand convulsed, seeking a Detonics CombatMaster or the Sting. His last conscious thought was, if he found either, he'd kill himself. Then darkness came to him again, a single burning tear escaped his right eye and slowly slid down the side of his face. Now, fully engulfed in the black void of his mind, the only movement was a continuing twitch of his right hand.

The Creator stepped back in the room. He, or more possibly "it," had dark grey skin, an elongated body and a small chest. The creature lacked muscular definition or visible skeletal structure and had no visible sex organs. The legs were shorter than in a human; the humerus and thighs appeared to be the same length as the forearms and shins.

Its head was unusually large in proportion to the body. There was no hair visible anywhere on the body, including the face. The face had no noticeable outer ears or nose, only small orifices for ears and nostrils. Its mouth was small. Its opaque black eyes were very large, but with no discernible iris or pupil. The creature stood about four feet tall, maybe slightly more, but only by an inch or two.

It stood for a long time staring at Rourke. The total lack of expression would have been disconcerting had Rourke been conscious to witness it. The only movement was isolated to the creatures head, periodically moving from side to side. On a human, it could have been interpreted as quizzical or thought-ful. Slowly, it laid its hand on Rourke's head, a gesture that could have been construed as gentle.

Had the creature been able to speak, or if John could have listened to its thoughts, he would have heard... *You are mistaken John Rourke.*

Author's Note

If you're like me, you've wondered about Rourke's Retreat; was it a real place or just part of Jerry's creative mind? According to Sharon Ahern, "Shortly after moving to Georgia in the late 1970s, we started exploring the beautiful countryside. We'd grab the kids, fill up the tank of our Ford LTD and take off for the day. One of these excursions took us into higher elevations and we discovered towns like Helen and Cleveland. Cleveland, by the way, is home to the original Cabbage Patch dolls where, if you're there at just the right time, you may be able to witness a birth. As we drove, a very distinctive mountain loomed off to our right. It wasn't the tallest mountain we'd seen in Georgia but, it was just different. For those of you who remember the beginnings of THE SURVIVALIST series, you might be interested in knowing that in order to get close to its base, the last paved road before you hit gravel is named Chambers Road. It just called out to us as the perfect place for the location of the Retreat. The actual name of that mountain is Mount Yonah or Yonah Bald and is located in the Chattahoochee National Forest."

Wikipedia credits the Spanish explorer Hernando de Soto who in the early 1500s searched the caves of Yonah for a lost Indian treasure; de Soto never found the treasure but in 1834 the village he and his men inhabited during the search was discovered by gold miners. To his credit though, de Soto did discover the Mississippi River.

Sharon added, "In THE SURVIVALIST, John Thomas Rourke actually bought the mountain and spent years renovating and supplying his hideaway. One thing most readers miss when they've talked to us about the Retreat is the fact that wherever a character traveled from point A to point B and there were stairs to take, for example, if they were going to a bedroom or the kitchen, we always had the same number of stairs throughout. Check out THE SURVIVALIST #3: The Quest. We did the same thing in some other books but it started with the Retreat. Writers do not remember everything and it pays to plan ahead, even with stairs."

Working with Sharon has been an ongoing educational process for me, not only has it been fun but I've learned some interesting facts. I'll share some of these with you from time to time. Not only was the location of the Retreat based in reality but... Jerry and Sharon always saw John Rourke with Charlton Heston's demeanor combined with the laconic voice of Clint Eastwood. There's a bit of trivia for you.

Bob

The Warrior's Last Stand, by Vic Roseberry
Copyright ©1980

Made in the USA
Lexington, KY
27 April 2015